MARIE B.

A Biographical Novel
by
TOM HUBBARD

KIRKCALDY
RAVENSCRAIG PRESS
2008

Ravenscraig Press
120 Commercial Street
Kirkcaldy KY1 2NX
Fife, Scotland

www.midoil.co.uk

Jacket Design by David McHutchon

ISBN 978 0 9556559 1 3

Typeset in house at the Ravenscraig Press
in Garamond

Printed in India by DEV Books

МАРИЯ КОНСТАНТИНОВНА БАШКИРЦЕВА
*1858   †1884

Preface and Acknowledgements

To use a term favoured by Irving Howe when he lectured on 'the biographical novel' at the Library of Congress some fifty years ago, what follows is a *distillation* of Marie's life and work. Here and there I have interpolated translations, or rather adaptations, of short passages from her actual journal, letters and notebooks.

In June 1993, when I came across Marie's self-portrait in a quiet corner of the Musée Jules Chéret in Nice, I felt its tragic power. A year later, working in Connecticut and still haunted by Marie's story, I conceived the idea for the present project.

Over the next decade, I introduced 'Marie' to students at Glasgow School of Art (during a one-day seminar on art and cities), the University of North Carolina at Asheville, Edinburgh College of Art and Edinburgh University Office of Lifelong Learning. The insights of these splendid people gave me the encouragement to pursue the project during a busy and often peripatetic career.

Special thanks are due to Prof. Louly Peacock Konz, a colleague in North Carolina and author of a scholarly monograph on Marie, and to Prof. Katalin Kürtösi (University of Szeged, Hungary), who drew my attention to the parody by Stephen Leacock.

I am indebted to David McHutchon of the Ravenscraig Press for taking on the book and seeing it through its final stages with enthusiasm and diligence. Jo Vorster and my daughter, Claire Hubbard, offered advice and assistance during the design and production process.

Parts of the work have appeared in earlier form in the magazines *Fife Lines*, *Markings* (Kirkcudbright) and *Rapid River Literary Digest* (Asheville). My thanks to the editors.

Prologue: The Debut of Marie B.

Unexpectedly, the sea was now turbulent. Unconcerned, the young girl raised her white skirts and bounded up the steps to the top deck. Her chaperone followed, less energetically if no more sedately, and muttered incomprehensible protests as she clutched first one railing then another.

The girl opened her arms, swirled around the deck, enraptured. 'I want to be part of all this. I want all this to be part of me.'

The older woman puffed.

'Mademoiselle, please. You will make a spectacle of yourself.'

'No I won't. The other passengers are too busy being sick.'

'But these young men are looking at you.'

'Let them. Am I not to be admired?'

The chaperone resumed her muttering, gestured with all fingers – a mistake, for she lost her balance, almost failing to flop down upon the nearest seat. The girl strode across the deck. As she passed, an elaborate youth raised his cane to his lips. The boat lurched and he chipped a tooth. The girl laughed, gazed across to the nearing shore.

She wondered at the texture of the cliff, which seemed not so much carved as piled with large brown and grey boulders. Counterpointing the irregular upper reaches of this frontage, there ran neat terraces built of flesh-tinted bricks. To and fro strolled the ladies and gentlemen of the city; if they looked out at sea from time to time, they glanced not at all at the boats approaching the harbour.

This high promenade was located at the extremity of Mont Boron. Two trees – two only, and at an interval from each other – rose from the topmost terrace, punctuating its wide curve of yellowish gravel. Criss-crossing this expanse were a pair of children, a boy and a girl, playing at tig, pursued by their nurse. This anxious person struggled with her parasol and her bonnet.

Beyond the terraces there spread a rich lawn, disrupted by outcrops of rock, and on the highest point was perched a building in mock-mediaeval style, curiously turreted and crenellated.

The weather suddenly calmed and a ray of sun struck the varying pinks of the parody castle. From the deck of the pleasure-

1

steamer came a cry of delight. It was the young woman in white; she was enjoying her life, and her chaperone couldn't understand why.

From another part of the deck came gasps of horror and indignation. A trio of middle-aged Italian women, obviously from steerage, had stolen up to the deck and had begun to dance. They had been drinking, and had linked their arms, not so much for choreography as for mutual support. The girl and her chaperone heard complaints that these persons had probably embarked at Ventimille and had overcome potentially obstructive officials by means of judiciously paced flirtation. The eldest possessed few teeth but was able to offset this by still eminently fulsome lips. As their dancing and giggling became increasingly frenetic, the three appeared all the sweatier and wrinklier. And more predatory.

The pallid young men, mostly English or American, baulked nervously at the invitations to join these sudden southern revels. Marie B. – the young woman in white – observed the various groupings and formations that were achieved or attempted. Her amusement was evident in the lower half of her face (and in the small gloved hand raised to her mouth), but her eyes were quizzical, piercing, intense.

Her concentration remained unbroken even when the legitimate passengers recoiled from a brisk affront by the toothless dancer. Stung to contempt for the elaborate young man and his rejection of her advances, the Italian made an obscene sign. Members of the crew, hastily summoned, grabbed the three women and pushed them below. Very shortly these ripe sirens would find it needful to exercise their charms on the harbour police and on those officers charged to escort them, none too gallantly, to the frontier.

Marie didn't lose a single gesture of the whole drama. She didn't even hear her chaperone vigorously assessing the scandalous nature of the *scene*, and the outcome (if *any*) of a complaint to this *clearly* corrupt and indolent steamship *company*.

At the Quai de la Douane, there ensued formalities and fussings between passengers and officials. As the genteel and the vulgar strove to misunderstand each other, Marie B. peered her last at the outrageous foreign females and imagined them as the three witches in Maestro Verdi's *Macbeth*. She pretended not to notice the Anglo-Saxon males who were noticing her. As her chaperone hailed a cab, and Marie followed at her own pace, the young men brayed loudly to each other, issuing challenges with a studied bravado. Who, they wondered, would be the first to climb that hill and reach the ruined château? Marie pouted and climbed into the cab.

They headed west. This was the cue for Mademoiselle Carignan, the chaperone, and she threw off a weight of words. It was important to avoid embarrassing *situations*. Mademoiselle Marie must remember that she belonged to an ancient and *noble* Russian family, but that certain members of that *family* had introduced 'uncomfortable *complications*' to its way of *life*. On no account - and here Marie knew what was coming - on no account must there be even the *passing* reference to her Uncle Georges and those debauches which had landed him in *prison*. He must not be mentioned, certainly not in public, and preferably not in private *either*. Perhaps she, Mademoiselle Carignan, had overstepped the *mark* by mentioning him now and to his niece at that, it was *imperative however* to heed her warnings however delicate she found it to *utter* them, it was *imperative* after all to remember that the family's *situation* was difficult ... well it would have been better (to put it as inoffensively as *possible*) had the family been more discreet in the past in its *utterances* if not in its *actions* and now the cab must be halted here in the old town of Nice *because* she, Mademoiselle Carignan, must enter the Cathedral of Ste.-Reparate to light a *candle* in memory of her poor *brother*, her brother the priest, unfrocked, but forgiven.

Marie just managed to restrain herself. At least she was relieved to alight from the cab, immured as she'd been with all that wretched babbling. She patted her brow with a handkerchief as Mademoiselle Carignan argued with the driver over the fare. *Quelle bourgeoise!* Was it really necessary to heed this tiresome woman's rigmarole and to follow her advice, in order one day to be received by the Russian ambassador in Nice, and thus to be able to enter society? The young girl even wished that it were her own misdeeds, and not those of her relations, which had led to the family's ostracism. She was too young, *hélas*, to have a personal history of deepest black; she wondered what sins Mademoiselle Carignan could ever be capable of committing, that she spent so long in the confessional.

In Marie's private ethic, the only deadly sin was mediocrity.

3

The young girl was already determined to become a serious scholar and artist. She would master all of Dante, Shakespeare and Goethe. She would sing the tragic heroines at La Scala. Perhaps, also, she would exhibit tableaux of modern life at the Paris Salons and sculpt graceful figures for the fountains and squares of Tuscan cities. To cultivate her voice was her greatest ambition to date, but might she not possess even nobler talents? Had not Leonardo exalted the visual arts above all others when he maintained that most of us would rather become deaf than blind?

To think that Mademoiselle Carignan was content to sit with her in the garden at a neat mimsy corner with tables and chairs of wicker, that she should be expected to flit her way through a bit of watercolour here and there, through a tedious English lesson book, through Italian (ha! now there's something!) if she was lucky, then to dottle inside with this shrivelled nettle of a woman, to peck away at the keys over some banal little *valse*.

Akh!

And now, Marie was dottling after Mademoiselle Carignan, along the nave of the Cathedral. The chaperone indeed lit a candle for her brother, then took the sudden notion to light a second. Just to be sure, she lit a third. She's terribly distracted, thought Marie. Now she's turning away, just as well, or she'll use up every candle in the building. Ah there, just as I suspected, she's off to the confessional. She'll be in there for hours, especially if she likes the priest's voice, the old hypocrite.

These followers of Rome! Marie, naturally, was of the Orthodox faith.

She contemplated the curtain of the confessional, and thought:

Why not? I'll be back in time.

So she escaped from the cathedral and into the Place Rossetti.

A fair was underway. Market-stalls were interspersed with open spaces where acrobats and jugglers began their acts, coaxing passers-by to linger. Already a huddle of men and boys had formed around a gaming table attended by a plump woman in her late forties; this was not quite the casino of Monte Carlo, but each player became excited at the prospect of winning a sugar-stick. At the centre of the square stood a fountain, in full spate; arrayed around it were the old wives with their trestle tables, laden with fish; these

4

women would sprinkle water on their wares to stop them drying out in the heat.

Marie approached the fountain and sang. She made swaying movements with her silk shawl, performed syncopations with her feet.

Rossigno che volà ...

The song, the singer, attracted the market women, who formed a circle round the young girl. The old ones began to dance. Marie was uttering those few words she knew of the Niçois dialect. The apple-sellers curtseyed and cried out to her:

Che bella regina!

Marie reddened with pleasure. The common people loved her so much, she didn't know why. She believed herself a queen indeed, but enjoyed talking to the people almost as if they were her equals. What an ovation she had earned from them today!

If I really were a queen, she thought, *my subjects would adore me.*

It was then, among her spectators, she saw *him.*

She was to look out for him, over the coming months, as he strolled past her home on the Promenade des Anglais. There would be an encounter at Baden-Baden where, in the presence of herself and her peers, he would remark on her power to amuse. She would fall in love with him, her first love, this elegant Englishman – the Duke of H. At least one Englishman was elegant! When she learned later that he kept a mistress, she was unperturbed; this made him even more desirable. How that man disdained all bourgeois convention. Just like Uncle Georges.

Today, at the fountain, she saw this wonderful creature for the first time. She was glad that her blushes could not be noticed, owing to her earlier excitation.

Nonetheless, her audience must have wondered at her sudden flight from the square and into the church. The Duke of H. swirled his cane and walked deeper into the old town, accompanied by a compatriot.

'I can persuade any woman to do what I want,' declared the Duke of H.

The other Englishman looked doubtful. 'Some women won't do what others will.'

'*Au contraire, mon ami,*' said the Duke of H. 'For me, they set no limits.'

5

And he puffed on his cigar.

Marie sprinted up the aisle. Which confessional was it? Oh yes. She swept aside the curtain, but there was another sinner within, and he wasn't pleased. *Oh no! Mademoiselle Carignan has returned to the Promenade des Anglais and I'll be in deep trouble with Grandpapa.* At last, however, she found the chaperone back at the candles; she was kneeling before them, in a trance.

The candles blazed more brightly than before: Mademoiselle Carignan had lit them all.

Marie, Marie B.: in their libraries, clever men would call her the Slav virgin who unknowingly announces the future, the seagull before the tempest. On the evening of her outing with and without Mademoiselle Carignan, Marie and her family found themselves once again uninvited by the philanthropic Vicomtesse de Veyrier. That lady, instead, had invited her own poor. Before the commencement of the performance at the opera, an assortment of ragged persons were urged on to the stage to offer their public thanks to their benefactress.

1
Border Crossing

A carriage in a cobbled square:
The muffled women, stepping out,
Wonder why they've been halted there,
Roused by a rough-accented shout.
The officer, his head unbare,
Demands to know what they're about.
The ladies through the drizzle stare
At this grim monumental lout.

Tapping her feet upon the stones,
Marie feels distant from all dance.
- 'Your papers!' – Ah, the affronted lass
Could show such papers, could unloose
The garnered volume of her nights
As if the ink flowed from her eyes …
Others draw the line where empires meet:
A one-line entry's all she'll need.

The raising of the frontier boom
Reveals no elegant avenue.
Beyond the insistent engine's steam
The east calls Mademoiselle Marie.
So she'll record this ritual show
Only in pigments of her prose;
The locomotive's long progress
To the autumn music of the steppes.

The brush succeeds the pen by stealth
Once the pert pilgrim's played her part.
She needs her father: *he is herself,*
The warring image of her art.
A woman forming through her words;
A painter learning how to see;
She'll pace the chamber of her birth,
Lands and the lineage of Marie.

2
The Journal of Marie B.

Gavronzi, July 1876

Paul looks at me quizzically all the time: it started when we met at the station. He has changed, but not really all that much; there is still something in his eye that once signified a big-brotherly threat to pull my hair. Now that we are both grown up (by our standards), the threat would be more a subtle means to embarrass me in company, his unique manner of showing how much he has come to admire and respect me.

On stepping out on to the platform you would recognise him at once – the way he has of raising an eyebrow, the turn-up of the mouth on the side of the eyebrow unraised. You would think he must have practised it – try doing the trick for yourself – but no, no, I think it must come to him naturally. For the first time I see him, my little Pavel, with a moustache; it is thick, but well-trimmed: not for him the unbarbered aspect of a Cossack.

(I thought of remarking that if there had been railway travel in Dante's time, it would have given the poet the idea for a circle of the *Inferno*. I said nothing, though, as I was not sure that my Paul would understand the allusion.)

'Well, little sister, you're quite a lady,' says he.

'And you're a trim young gentleman,' says I. 'I hope you're a gentleman in every sense, for the young ladies hereabouts must everyone of them be sighing for you.'

He laughs slyly.

'The young ladies hereabouts will be gnashing their teeth.'

'How so?' I asked him.

'In envy of ... Marie ... and her French ways. Akh! Masha, when I drop in on you in France, totally unexpected – '

'Don't, Paul ... Pavel: warn me well in advance.'

'When I drop in on you in France, totally unexpected, I would like to meet some nice French girls. You can introduce me.'

'Don't count on me to be your go-between, Monsieur Paul.'

As the conversation was progressing, if progressing is the right word, we were rumbling across an uneven road as the Ukraine parted on both sides to receive me. Paul had shoved me through the station-house, a battered box of a building between the platform and

8

the dusty square of the hamlet. At a desk behind a grille sat an old fellow, tapping absently at the telegraph. His stained cap lay at an angle, touching the tip of an incredibly hairy ear. His beard seemed to have sprouted from his red, carbuncled nose. I spotted gobbets of bread lodged in his whiskers: he carried his food cupboard, as it were, about with him. I itched for a pencil and paper, but in my excitement at coming 'home' I had stupidly packed them deep within my trunk. At such times, I have only memories and words – mere words! – to go on.

If I were the dedicated artist which I mean to be, I would *always* carry something sharp with me, to prick the blood out of myself and sketch upon my skin.

As the droshky rocked along, I caught sight of a wooden pole with a roofed board upon it – a shrine perhaps, or a sign-post, I don't know at this stage as I've become so unfamiliar with my native land. There is so much to rediscover and record – and, one day, the Salon will bear witness to the results!

'Who is that?' I asked Paul, having observed a hooded figure swaying by the post.

'Ha! It's that old witch, Alyona. Peasant woman, about a hundred, probably more. Sets herself up as a soothsayer. Cunning old beggar, if you ask me. I'd ha' thought you'd remember her. Apparently she informed one of our servants, and it somehow got out to mother, that I'd develop like everyone else, but you would become a star. Tosh! The truth is that you and I together, dear sister, will become a constellation.'

'Why is she making that weird dance, Pavel? For it looks like a dance to me.'

'Dance! She'd grace any ballroom, wouldn't she? Akh, it's just one of her favourite spots, over there. But she gets rich pickings, I'll tell you – see, it's at the crossroads – traditional venue for your prophetesses. The yokels passing by don't have much, but she can winkle out of them what little they have. Probably scares them with tales of hell if they don't cough up.'

'Perhaps she gives them good value, if she's worth so much! What, really, do you think she tells them?'

'Beats me! Only they would be able to understand her, that's for sure. She talks their dialect. Gibberish, if you ask me. Where are my matches?'

I took a quick glance behind me as he fumbled in his pockets. Then I stared ahead, in what I thought would be the direction of our manor.

'Father says she should be whipped.' Paul lit his cigarette, threw the match behind him. If he had not been so nonchalant, I would almost have thought that our father had ordered him to immolate the dry old hag. The faint glow of a near-spent match might have been enough to do just that.

'That's terrible, Pavel. Even if she deserves it.'

'What? Oh, our faded belle, you mean? The countess of stale urine? No, she shouldn't be whipped. She should be seduced instead. Only don't ask me to do it.'

My brother laughed, threw away his cigarette, lit another.

'I wish you wouldn't smoke, Paul. *C'est dégoûtant.*'

'My dear Masha, need I say it again, there will be no call for these fine French manners around here. There's no-one here who isn't as coarse and common as the muzhik in that field.'

The fellow in question had dropped his rake, or whatever it was, and clutched his cap to his chest, bowing.

'I'm only joking of course, Masha. We have our own style, let's just put it that way.'

I thought that my interminable journey was almost over. In front of us, rusty iron gates were parting: we swept past, between two columns bedabbled with moss. On each of these I noticed an urn, or something like an urn. If the vehicle had collided with the stonework – which was quite possible, in view of the recklessness of its career – the whole structure might well have fallen on top of us.

In a second, of course, I could take in much and that included the likelihood that we had still had some way to go before Father would greet me on these dimly-remembered steps. The birch-lined drive was impressive, I suppose, but I was clutching the side of the carriage as it squelched along the track. Paul – or Pavel as I should be calling him – let out an oath as we lodged in a puddle. Fortunately there were a couple of fellows about, carrying wood and piling it by a shed. Pavel ordered them over. One of them appeared to be deaf, or perhaps just stupid; the other one had to relay Pavel's commands to this fellow, so that took up much time.

'You'll need to be patient, little Masha; nothing here happens quickly, except drunkenness and pregnancy.'

10

Eventually we resumed and as the woodland gave way to a rough lawn, we settled into a jog-trot. And there it was before me, my old home, somewhat yellower and shabbier than I had remembered it.

There was Father! He was smoking, nervously, and gazing at me with what I fancied was a blend of affection and mistrust. We embraced, but he didn't want to make a fuss. Neither did I: I won't encourage him to be presumptuous.

'Mother looks after you well, I see.' (His little eyes are quite penetrating, but I'm more than a match for him).

'And so does Mlle Carignan, my governess,' I said in a mock-conspiratorial tone. 'She looks after me too well, Father, so I would find your neglectfulness oddly refreshing.'

'Hum. How was your journey?'

He asks banal questions with an air suggesting his awareness of their precise degree of banality.

'Considerably pleasanter without Mlle Carignan. She was in great consternation at the station, when she was told that she would have to follow in a separate carriage. She dared not argue with Paul - Pavel - though, when he insisted on a private drive with his darling little sister. Her expression was most amusing; some time I must sketch it for you. But I fear that we shall have the pleasure of her company in due course.'

'At table we'll place her beside Rabkin, the old dancing-master,' says Paul. 'They can out-bore each other.'

Father interrupted; it was the first sign of animation on his part.

'The border! What happened at the border? You crossed at Eydtkühnen, yes?'

Why does he suddenly come out with this, I'm thinking.

'Well, actually, father, it was terrible. The guards were frightfully boorish. And we had just enjoyed a charming time at the inn on the Prussian side. Well, I enjoyed it anyway; Carignan just sat there as if she were in her church. There was a terrace, and they had lit lanterns because of the fog. We saw lights in the east, too, and they had haloes round them. I said to Mlle Carignan that there was Holy Russia. She only harrumphed, as is her way; no sense of occasion. But the guards, oh the guards!'

'Yes, the guards, well?'

'They clearly had no idea how to treat people of quality. Has my country come to this, father, that the servants of the Tsar are such clodpoles?'

'My dear Masha – or Marie if you prefer – His Imperial Majesty is having problems with … people of quality.'

'Mother told me nothing of this.'

'Mother, for God's sake! Your mother wouldn't. You people in the west have no idea. You never have, and you never will. Damn it girl, it's these Nihilists, don't you be getting mixed up with them.'

'Nihilists?'

'Sons of landowners they are, daughters too, some of 'em. If it was only a lot of talk-talk at their universities, about progress, science and all the rest of it, fine. But we hear rumours of conspiracies, guns, bombs. Oh, it'll happen some day if the authorities don't crack down in time. Then who will be dangling from the end of a rope? Not your usual vodka scum of the stews and the ditches. It'll be the lovely young people, that's who it'll be, the people of beauty made ugly by republicanism and atheism and all the rest of it.'

'Father, you really sound as if you cared. Beauty!'

'No, you couldn't have anything to do with them, Masha, not with your art and your literature and all the rest of it. These people would abolish such things.'

'Art and literature, father! So they're important to you, father, are they?'

He looked embarrassed; doubtless I will love him dearly when he's like that.

'Yes … well … I suppose they are. My generation had ideals … once'

'Don't these people have ideals?'

'Nihilists? Think of the word … they believe in nothing, girl. For them there is no God; we are but slime from the pit.'

I was about to remark that the present condition of our estate suggested an imminent descent into the said pit. I held my peace, though. I don't mind being offensive, but I won't allow myself to be pompous.

What an entry this has been!

3
Alyona the Spae-Wife

The girl Marie, Masha, had become increasingly skilled at giving her governess the slip. She rose early: to relish the moonlight, she had opened her shutters, but had nevertheless slept well; now, with the dawn, she wanted to enjoy the sunlight on the same view.

She leaned at the window for some minutes. The ranks of birch reached out into a haze of grey, green and brown; each tree seemed to rise in a tension between a brisk, military uniformity and a desire to bend and curve more or less in a generally upward direction. Carefully and quietly Marie made her toilette, descended the grand staircase, struggled with a heavy door ... and was out.

She decided to avoid the main avenue or indeed any road by which she had arrived yesterday. The long train journey, with its regular rhythms and predetermined route; the scheduled meetings with her brother and father; the condition of guardianship and protection – she wanted to avoid all that on this, the first day of adventure.

She selected a footpath through the park. Its windings might eventually settle towards one point or another: she neither knew nor cared about that. The summer light filtered through the leaves, and there was a dappling upon the stream before her: she crossed this by a rough, narrow bridge of logs, stretching out her arms to keep her balance. If she had fallen in, perhaps she would not have minded; she might even have emerged, dripping and laughing, to welcome such a beginning to her expedition.

The way through the wood was rough and uneven; at times she stumbled over clumps and hillocks. She risked squelching into a ditch or being scratched by brambles. In spite of her sheltered upbringing, she seemed to have an instinct that kept her ankle untwisted and her neck unbroken. At last she came to the boundary wall: where now?

The dilapidation of the estate worked in her favour. At several points, the upper part of the wall had crumbled. The heaps of fallen masonry allowed for an easy scramble to the other side. Any Nihilist could have made the crossing in reverse, got into the manor and murdered her father – but such determination would have been born not of necessity but of will, and a strange will at that, as her father was hardly the most powerful landowner in all the Russias, and his notoriety was surely only that of a social, rather than a political nature? Ostracism, yes; assassination, no?

Yet the family was hardly obscure locally, so when she found herself approaching the village, its inhabitants seemed to know her. Here was a fine young lady, after all. Perhaps the rumours had spread – the master's daughter had arrived from a faraway land where all the roofs were made of gold and the seas yielded such enormous fish that no-one needed to starve.

The peasants had lined up on either side of her, each of them bowing in turn as she passed. She thought comically of cards or dominoes toppling over each other according to cue.

Not one of them uttered a word.

A few of the buildings seemed to be grander – comparatively speaking – than the others, but their turrets and spires were fashioned from the same awkwardly-hewn trunks that made up the village as a whole. There appeared here to be a sort of municipality; as for that pile perched at an angle to the square, it was obviously the church, judging by the sadly leaning crucifix atop its battered dome. One would not venture too near, she thought, in case the cross collapsed and dashed out one's brains.

The bolder peasants – they were not many – stretched out dry claws to receive alms. Marie flickered a few kopeks into each one.

They must not sense any fear from me, she thought. *I have no fear. In fact, it is all quite amusing, even refreshing after these uniformed boors at the frontier ...*

A faint memory of the authorities' paranoia, as outlined by her father yesterday, came and went. These cowering people could not possibly be mobilised against their betters! No – but her father was right about the beautiful young ones, surely. It would be they who would rise up and bring down the Tsar. They would resemble her, wouldn't they? After all, she was herself beautiful.

At last she felt the peasants' attentions to her to be a little tiresome and she made for a narrow lane that straggled off the main street and petered out into a footpath between mould-pocked fences. The folk became agitated, crossed themselves.

They are concerned for me, poor things. But I can look after myself.

She cast a pile of coins behind her and the people scrambled upon the ground. She continued her way through a field and into a forest. Birds chirped as she followed the up-and-down path. It was sunny and pleasant, at first. Ten minutes later, the path was obscured by fallen branches. The earth was sodden, with a layer of mist above it. Something appeared to be watching her through the undergrowth. It was moving. With the fascination of those suddenly attracted to danger, she tramped closer to the figure. It was a tall cross and seemed to lurch towards her as if it were yet another beggar seeking alms. Where the eyes would be, there were white things crawling.

She shrieked.

She stumbled upon the overturned markers of graves. The name-boards had rusted and rotted away from their posts; some would still have been decipherable, but most of the lettering had either been eaten away or was obscured by dark, spreading stains. It was as if cancerous tumours persisted in mocking and murdering the dead. In the darker corners of this abandoned sepulchre, there were spots of phosphorescence, and there was a smell suggesting the imminent eruption of the horrors below.

The neglected graves seemed to become more densely packed as she made her uneasy progress through the wood. The tumuli appeared to swell in the mist. It was as if the very guts of the earth would burst before collapsing in on itself, sucking in all objects and creatures lacking a secure hold on the surface.

Marie took a handkerchief from her bosom and covered her face; she soon felt, though, that she needed to have both hands free, should she fall in this terrible place.

She froze.

From a heap of logs there glistened and slithered a reptilian shape. *Are they poisonous in the Ukraine?* she asked herself, stupidly. Its liquid movement did not, however, turn threateningly in her direction. There was a trickling, melting sound, almost risibly high-pitched.

She tripped and fell on the mess. Her screams echoed through the wood. Then a ray of sun lit up the scene. Gigantic, obscene fungi were clustered around her, swaying in their impertinent ascendancy and decay. Tumescent, bulbous, or in pleated, curtain-like folds, they cast their spores into the mean air.

They would all end up as the black, clammy stuff which stuck to Marie's clothes and fingers.

She followed the rays as if they were noble liberators. Another path appeared. She had no idea whence it had come or whither it was going, but it promised escape from all that dreadful momentary life which battened upon death.

Emerging from the ghastly forest, Marie sensed that her whole being was polluted: she needed not so much a bath as a baptism. The ground rose in a series of knolls, and in one of their dips she found a small pool – not fresh, but not quite stagnant, because of the tiny stream running through. She immersed as much of herself as was possible in the shallows. She dared not strip, but cast water over both skin and clothes. At times she became frustrated at the stubbornness of the filth upon her; she ground her teeth, wept. How dare this happen to her.

The stains and the odour were by no means removed, but at least she felt a little better after her quasi-ablutions. The ground levelled out: she found herself on a wide plateau, and the beauty of her native land was there before her.

Her tears were the gentle ones of a being first awed, then subdued.

Irregular patches of field and forest stretched below and beyond. The sun picked out threads of river, as well as the domes and spires of distant churches.

She knelt, kissed the ground.

A numbness succeeded: ten minutes passed before she came out of her trance and was able to consider immediate practicalities. She noticed, to her right, what seemed like a pile of logs: coming closer, she saw that it was a broken fence marking the beginning or end of a track. She followed it, taking no thought for its destination, if any. Renewed curiosity had overtaken fear.

The track widened, with ample foliage on either side. This might have been just another pleasant summer stroll, and for the first time she felt a certain affinity between this and her many rambles – albeit chaperoned – along dry, reddish paths in the uplands between Nice and Grasse. However, hunger and fatigue gradually overcame her, and she was torn between resting at a verge or pressing on in the hope of encountering a peasant with a cart.

16

The line of trees ended first on one side, then on another, and there appeared to be a crossroads ahead – at last she might be able to get her bearings. But the scene was as unfamiliar as anything she had witnessed that morning. Then she caught sight of a wooden pole, with a board on top; a shrine, perhaps, or a signpost, and a hooded figure swaying beside it. Marie felt drawn towards the ancient hag.

Here lassie, bonny lassie, a bit siller fir Alyona; bless her speerit and her sowel, fir they're baith destined fir the lang darg ayont daith.

It was Alyona, whom she had passed on this spot the day before, at whom her brother had laughed in his studied urbanity. That evening, Paul had told her that the peasants called the greasy old thing a *spae-wife*. She'd tell your fortune for a few kopeks; if you wanted a blissful, trouble-free future, make it a few roubles instead. Just like these new insurance policies, so called, that you could buy in the West.

The taloned arm was outstretched. There was hardly any flesh upon it, indeed hardly any skin. Marie shuddered. If this shrunken creature suddenly became naked, surely what was left of her body would be transparent. One would see bones, veins, perhaps even the tattered tissue falling off her. Under the hood, as the head rose tortoise-like to the sun, appeared the face of a skull.

There were not enough teeth for grinning. One eye still swivelled, red and viscous, in its socket. The other seemed to be made of opaque glass, in which one would fear to see one's reflection. The old woman drew her long nails down her face, as if to remove a mask.

Marie screamed.

In her terror she dropped the coins which she had intended to give the creature. Alyona lurched forward, grabbed the money, the arm somehow placing it meltingly within the darkest interstices of her robe.

Look east, lassie, look east.

Since Marie's arrival in this land, her most wondering gazes had been in an easterly direction. She felt both fascinated and chilled by Alyona's injunction.

Look east, lassie, ti the cowpit chaipel, and the planks that lead inti the loch.

- And what must I do there, old woman?

17

If old woman you are, she thought. Marie was gradually regaining her composure, but a new uneasiness had entered her life. Still, she felt somewhat emboldened again. She must hear the creature out.

Ye maun tak a bit boatie that's tied up there, hen. There'll be naebody else aboot, juist the Deevil and his hingers-on, but they're ilkawhaur, sae there's nae differ.

- Did you say the Devil, old wife?

The Deevil? Ay, I did that, hen. I ken him fine, he wis my fancy-man yince. Dinna you be feart o him. He's an auld saftie, 'cept whaur it maitters. Ay, he wis a braw luver, hen; there's that lume upon him growes sae reid, ye'd no be led astray in the daurk!

Alyona the spae-wife chuckled with all the ugliness of which she was capable, and more. Marie shuddered, felt nauseous.

Whit's the matter wi ye, lassie? Dinna you come doun wi somethin, mind.The folk hereabouts are that ignorant they blame aa their diseases on me. Aiblins whan they and I were younger, and some o thaim cowpit me on the fly, likes, I gien thaim the pox, but thon's a lang time syne, and they're aa deid – baur the Deevil, and nane cuid pleisure a lassie like him.

Marie felt that she should interrupt these ramblings and learn more about her future, for she was beginning to half-believe in the powers of the creature.

- Tell me, ... grandmother, how shall I die?

What had come into her? Why did she ask that? Why didn't she inquire about her impending greatness – as painter, writer or musician, or all three? Why this sudden curiosity about morbidity, especially after the squalid experiences of a day which had begun merely as the most recent naughty escape from her chaperone?

- Will I die by my own hand?

No! Had it come to this – words were spouting from her lips before she realised what she was saying. Worse still, the old woman raised her head again, and the sun – though now in decline – lit up the wormy horror of the face.

Na, na, lassie. Dinna you dae that, hen, else they'll yird ye here at the crossgates, deep under but no sae deep that ye'll no be hauntin puir Alyona fir aye. Fir they're aye here aboot me, my dearie-o, the sel-murtherers, makkin sic a stishie aroon me as gin I were the yin that garred thaim dae it. It's as I'm tellin ye, hen; Alyona the spae-wife gets blamed fir aathing. Ye'd think they'd hae

18

burnt me bi nou – ay, and sae they wad, but they're ower feart ti lay a finger on me.

As indeed I would be, thought Marie, as if guessing the meaning of the warlock's ferlie speech.

I'll tell ye hou ye'll dee, lassie.

Marie wasn't sure, now, that she really wanted to know. But the old wife continued. Marie felt numb: she was somehow as unwilling to stir as to stay.

It's the loch, lassie, you gang there as I telt ye.

- You mean the lake with the chapel and the boat? Am I going to drown there? (If I go there, she thought, it will indeed be the suicide she's warned me against. The old witch contradicts herself. I smell evil in it, whatever it means.)

Na, hen, ye'll no droun. But ye'll gang in as the watter-lassie, and ye'll come oot as the ice-lassie.

Marie had more than an inkling of Alyona's meaning; with a weird rapidity she was picking up the peasant dialect.

I hope I never find myself speaking it, she thought later. But at present she recalled, bizarrely, one or two childhood tales, as told by a former nurse, or perhaps even by her mother. Did she hear them in infancy, here in Gavronzi, all these years ago? Surely not – how could she remember that far back? Or in Nice? A few of the women who had looked after her were Russian, perhaps even Little Russian.

'*A lassie there wis, lowpt inti the watter:*
She gaed in Rusalka, and cam oot Snyegúrochka.'

That was it! Now the spae-wife was chanting it – well, croaking it. What a blood-curdling rasp in the words, now rising painfully in her own consciousness.

'*She gaed in Rusalka, and cam oot Snyegúrochka.*'

And so it was that Rusalka, the water-maiden, singing lonely to the moon, plunged to the depths, and rose again as Snyegúrochka, the girl of snow and ice. Was it the moon that froze her, somewhere in the isolated steppe?

And ye'll wander lang, as the bluid-wumman.

Alyona's abrupt words broke her reverie. Blood? Blood? The sunlight was no more. The mist of the marshlands was gathering fast, the expanse of Holy Russia was narrowed to the crossroads, to the tilted post and the swaying prophetess.

19

- Blood, grandmother, blood? Do you see anyone else there? A man? Men? My paint, my ink, are they mixed with blood?

Her questions baffled her even as she uttered them.

Ye'll wander lang as the bluid-wumman, and sit at last in the shaddas.

That was it. Alyona said no more. In fact Alyona herself was no more as the mist swirled and thickened around her. Marie continued to stand, utterly immobile, as new images – some vivid, others vague – formed themselves before her inner eye.

She had forgotten which of the four ways was the best one for home.

The mist cleared. Alyona the spae-wife was gone. Marie saw a dim light on the horizon – a lodge, fallen masonry, gates. Her two men, her father and her brother, would be waiting for her; figures – probably the search party – appeared on the road, heading in her direction. She stepped decisively towards her Ukrainian home and whatever else lay ahead of her.

4
The Enchanted Lake

... Nice? The Cathedral, and the candles flickering, going out one by one? No, there's a path, losing itself in the undergrowth, which I shall never follow ... and these are eyes appearing and disappearing through the darkening leaves ... I'm afraid ... no, they're the eyes of Mlle Carignan only, not of wolves surely, she's angry that I keep escaping from her. Or a werewolf, she's turned into a werewolf and it's a hall of mirrors endlessly reflecting her absurd peering pince-nez. Her finger wagging, her umbrella wagging, no, birches in the breeze ... I must catch that dappling effect ... a painter I must be, and put down these patches of shapes and colours ... put them down when I see them, freshly, not afterwards, because memory will dissolve – will clarify too much –

Not the Place Rossetti this – how ridiculous! But a sighing from the east ... is that water? A fountain? What are the sighs and ripples saying?

Che bella regina!

I must sing to them: what shall I sing to them? A musician I must be, my harp tall and looming over my palette ... *how dreadful it would be to become deaf, to lose the wind in the branches, a brook babbling, a girl's soft voicing of a name ...*

Rossigno che volà!

Not nightingales these – cranes? They talk, in the village, of cranes, cranes, strange spirits lamenting for all the Russias, lamenting for Europe as well if all goes badly, as is feared these days ... but the village knows nothing of *that*, of course.

Wolves? Werewolves? I should not be here. The old hag at the crossroads has lured me here ... she may be a wolf, a bear, a fish ... the spider in that web: look through the web ... a hut! The moonlight! I'll shelter there.

A Cathedral this, a little one; neglected – no candles, an ikon or two rotting, the paint flaking ... how can they let that happen to a picture? Are the Nihilists responsible for such an outrage? No, they wouldn't bother about an out-of-the-way place like this; *let it sink into history*, they'd say.

The little chairs before the altar: I cannot explain this. The Catholics only are seated, not us ... Were they brought here for the old who can stand no longer? Little, old chairs, rough from the carpenter's hand, rough as the sitter's backside ... Ostend! Ostend! The Kursaal – I'm in my early teens (not so long ago really) swaying seductively on those elegant round-backed chairs ... mother is drinking a seltzer for her fluttery stomach; Mlle Carignan, less refined, drinks a glass of Belgian beer. The café is busy it's an enormous hall effeminate fat men waddle from the gaming room spending their losings on large slices of chocolate cake they pat their napkins on the brown dribble descending the corners of their mouths fat men with mouths full of shit.

The Promenade: looking towards England: how many languages are spoken on this beach? I heard two men behind me, walking back to the Kursaal; neither of them was *him*, *him*, the Duke of H., worse luck.

'Hey, look, Sir Edward, git a load of them ladybugs!'

Disgusting. He sprinkles his cigar-ash on these sweet little blobs of red with black spots.

'Lay-dee-bugs? Lay-dee-bugs, Mr Westhoven?'

'Sure, Sir Edward. Ain't you seen 'em afore? Don't you have them critters in ole England?'

'Mr Westhoven, please. We do not call them 'ladybugs'. Frightful name!'

'Well, whaddaya call 'em then? Peers of the realm?'

'Ladybirds, Mr Westhoven. We call them ladybirds.'

Pause.

'Well, darn it, Sir Edward, they doan look like ladies to me, nor birds neither.'

Another pause.

'Hey, young lady, whaddif I called you a young ladybird, ha! ha!'

Naturally I ignored him – pretended I knew no English. I heard pathetic little sounds and could have sworn that he crunched some of these insects underfoot. I couldn't bear to look. The beast.

I continue along the sand, gazing at the German Ocean: perhaps the Duke of H. is beyond, drinking whisky in his Highland castle ... oh, I am lonely here, singing to the moon ... the moon, the moon, and the distant wail of bagpipes, the deer standing proud on the Scottish crag, firs behind and below all the way to a loch shining in the night ... like something out of Walter Scott ...

... I would be a hind, pursued by the Duke, he'd aim his rifle and ... blood dissolves in the German Ocean, in the Russian lake ... the white of the moonlight tashed with red ...

I'm not afraid of this lake. A boat – yes! How it bobs at the jetty, by that line of planks creaking in the slightest breeze ... is it safe to walk out? Who cares about safety? Not me ... how I foot it delicately ... oh, there, nasty: the boat will be more reliable than the jetty ... there, I'm in: I did that with such style, didn't I? An artist, and a lady artist especially, meets all danger with panache.

If Mlle Carignan were here, she'd insist on getting in with me, and we'd sink ... the pig she is! I could glide in this, with my parasol, as if I were on the Seine ... no, that's too genteel. This – do I need to remind myself – is Russia! And there, as I lean over (akh! careful!) is not Marie, but Masha ...

Masha ... Masha ... with her diadem of snow: the bastard daughter of Winter and Spring. The Sun, offended by their coupling, refused to warm the village which suffered thereafter from blizzards. She must be protected from the Sun and remains in the forest, but, no, she must be among mortals and their dancing. So an old peasant couple adopt her. She grows up and, alas, for all her love of revelry, she cannot love men ...

... Until she meets Mizgir, a lad of rough ways except for his words of adoration for her ... Alone and sad, wandering in the forest, she invokes her mother Spring, who garlands her with flowers as the earth awakens, as you too awaken, Masha ...

You accept Mizgir, but as the Tsar Berendei blesses your union, the clouds part and the Sun beams down upon you ... you melt, you ripple, dissolve in these dark fathoms ...

5
A Raven of the Steppe. Brother and Sister.

'So, little sister, you're quite an amphibian, or so you thought! You belong anyway to a remarkable species. You must, with a brother like me. But you don't float very well.'

Marie's expression, hazy as it was, told him to be quiet or she would visit unspeakable vengeance upon him.

'Now, Masha, don't look at me like that! You should be grateful that your loving brother arrived in time.'

'With the help of some of your village souls,' Marie added. As soon as she had regained consciousness, she had been determined to make a full recovery. Meantime, though, she was enjoying all the attention, and relished the thought of Mlle Carignan's likely discomfiture. Indeed, the governess was alternately flittering and fuming from anteroom to anteroom, unable to berate Marie's father and brother for their neglect (they were her superiors, after all, though foreign), and equally unable to berate her errant charge. On her first day at Gavronzi, Marie had instructed Paul never to admit Mlle Carignan to her private quarters, and her brother was more than happy to keep 'that tiresome French frump' at even greater distance since Marie's rescue from the lake.

The governess – who still considered herself to be also chaperone – was finding that, in this dreadful part of the world, her movements were more restricted than those of Marie. It was an intolerable role-reversal, but what could she do? If she protested, brother and sister could telegraph to mother that daughter had been dangerously neglected by a woman who, really, was no more than a servant, and should be dismissed forthwith. The whole trip was a mistake; the wretched girl had at last found, in her brother, a reliable ally.

Paul ... Pavel formed his unique eyebrow and corner-of-the-mouth expression, chuckled at his co-conspiratorial sister.

'Yes, well, I must admit that if those malodorous old boors weren't kindling a fire nearby, it would have taken longer to fish you out. But – oof – what a reek came off them, and you weren't all that fragrant yourself, Masha. What was down there, by the way? Didn't you have time to look before you passed out? And I thought you were so dedicated to the pursuit of knowledge. Still, don't be in

24

any hurry to repeat your experience; it was as unpleasant to me as it was to you, as it disturbed me from the perusal of a rather wild French novel translated by one of Kiev's more, er, exotic booksellers.'

'I regret interrupting your international literary education. But do shut up, little brother. Is my father about?'

'Oh, him, he's been in Kiev, our dear metropolis, visiting an old flame. I believe he's on his way home; we telegraphed him about your adventure. I must ask him if we really share a mother, or if you were the result of his affair with a mermaid.'

Since her arrival from the west, Marie could not decide whether to take offence or to relish her brother's unparalleled impudence. Now, saved from the lake and gaining a little strength every day, she found comfort in his bedside manner.

'Pavel dear, don't you ever take anything seriously?'

'Ha! Since when have *you* done just that?'

'I asked the first question. Maybe you should study to become a doctor.'

'Our father wouldn't allow it. You know it's not the calling of a gentleman. Would you really want me to become the village quack? Ugh! Draining the pus from the feet of the yokels!'

'You would find society patients in St Petersburg. You've been nursing me well.'

'Then maybe I should become a nurse, not a doctor, but a nurse is not the calling of a lady.'

He put on the voice of a bossy, bustling female.

'So then, you can hear what a terrible lady I'd be, Masha!'

Marie chuckled in spite of herself.

'Now that I've performed for you, Masha, and answered your question with a display of my irredeemable dilettantism, it's my turn to repeat *my* question: since when have *you* been serious about anything?'

'Oh Pavel, my dear, as I get better, I become more serious than I've ever been in my life.'

She had suddenly sat up in bed as she uttered these words. Pavel was taken aback by her vehemence.

'Yes, Pavel, I'm not playing any more.'

'You want to be an artist, then, Masha; it's settled; but what is that but play?'

She raised her hands, tousled her hair, let it shake free.

'We play best at what we've worked at.'

'And what is that supposed to mean? Play is play. Shush! Here comes the servant. Don't let her see you like that. Every little mannerism in the house, it feeds the chatter of the kitchen, and in turn of the village, and our father would learn about it from one of the wise old soaks he meets in the stables and ... worse places.'

'My father does not consort with common people.'

'You'll learn soon enough. There are the male ones, with whom he shares the pleasures of the bottle, and the female ones, with whom he shares the pleasures of the bed. You know so little about our father, Masha.'

'I'm a match for my father, Paul; you'll see. And for you, too, Paul, or Pavel, whoever you are, I'll show you what a tough little goblin I can be.'

'You certainly survived a major ducking, I'll give you that. You must be a water goblin, a vodnik as the riff-raff call them. You're probably more than a match for the fair Alyona, even.'

'I'll survive more than the lake, brother; survive and thrive. Listen: I had a dream last night – no, don't sneer, it wasn't delirium, I assure you. I was high above the earth, with a harp in my hand, but I could draw no music from it: only silence in the steppes of heaven. Then I rose higher, and saw a wide horizon of green and purple mountains, through clouds of all colours – blue, red, yellow, silver, gold. The whole spectrum was before me. Then everything went grey, and then resplendent again, as I rose higher and higher. It was then that I was able to make my harp sing, and I myself sang with it. Far below there was suspended a bright scarlet ball, the earth.'

'Not to worry, Masha. You'll get better: someone else will inherit such nonsense from you.'

6

A Raven of the Steppe. Father and
Daughter: The Journal of Marie B.

August, 1876

... It's all becoming clearer. Pavel was right. My father is indeed a reprobate and probably beyond redemption. And he has the effrontery to call Pavel degenerate!

I am tense: I attempt to brace myself for inevitable further unpleasantness – whatever form that may take – with my father. Already, we have had to meet at the extremes. I was too long in my bed, shivering my way through convalescence; he, never coming up to visit me, slouched in an armchair in the conservatory, mopping up the best vodka he could find in Kiev, reminiscing to the plants about the good old days.

Extremes, I say? We are, after all, Russian. A father and daughter such as us must obtain the final measure of each other. In both of us there is a combination of great strength and greater weakness: the one is intimately related to the other.

What is – was – his strength?

He has told me, in a rare moment of placidity (which in his case is also lucidity, and when we were not arguing or at least not bickering) – that as a young man he was much waylaid from his studies at the university. That much I could have guessed already. But I was astonished at the nature of the waylaying. Nights in the taverns – understandable, I concede, for a young fellow living innumerable versts from an isolated estate, enjoying the freedoms of a large city (hardly Paris, though, or even Nice!) However, on one occasion in his cups, he'd got into a crowd of fellow-students none of whom he'd ever met before.

'I'd usually consorted with a group of junior officers but they'd begun to bore me with their tales of conquest – in the bed, that is; you never heard about the field or even pistols at dawn. I was never going to be a force to be reckoned with in the army, so that was why I was at the university, though I had no idea how I was going to become a force to be reckoned with there either. So this new lot, they called 'emselves German idealists or something like that, could never fathom what they were on about most of the time with their dialectic this and that. But they had their plans to waken up Russia and I'm a patriot, y' know.'

He drained his glass, refilled it, and went on.

'Well, I'd simply lurched from one set of talkers to another. One of 'em had this thing about a Frenchie fellow who believed in the noble savage or other. You'll find savages a-plenty down our way, I told 'im, but there's nary a noble one among 'em. Still, when you're young, a lot of that kind of stuff goes to your head and it's pitiful when you don't have a clear enough head to figure it out in all its cold detail. I'm not a details man, me – the vague, fleeting sensation, let me capture that – Masha – and I'm a happy man.'

He sought further vague, fleeting sensation in his glass.

'There was a girl. Not your mother, she came many girls later, God blast her! Sorry, Masha. Well, that girl became Russia for me. My high thoughts became focused on her. Worship her, worship my country! There's where all your dialectic should be tending. She was flesh and blood, b' God she was, and you shouldn't turn a woman into a symbol.'

I nodded guarded agreement.

'One night my new cronies and I were tumbling out of some God-awful den intent on some secret mission, God knows what, for I hardly knew m'self, but it was to be patriotic in nature and they'd sort of convinced me we'd become heroes, we'd be saving the country from dark forces and all the women would be at our feet as a result. I now know that *they* were the dark forces. One fellow told me we'd just consecrated our plan in his favourite *Hof* – his word for a tavern, I ask you. I told 'im, why d'ye use them Frenchie German words if you're such a great Russian!

'I should have thought that through, but that's me, I don't do thought, see? Well, we didn't get far. We rondy-vooed with three chaps in a cemetery – creepy they were, too, in black capes and hoods. Dammit, I want to see a fellow's face, size 'im up, find out if he's a good egg or not. So we all takes this zigzag way up and down steps, across railway bridges, down alley-ways with only a flicker of light from the odd lamp here and there, and we arrive at an important-looking building – one of His Imperial Majesty's government buildings, no less! And we're supposed to be saving Russia!

'Then, from a dark courtyard, the police pounced. We were holed up in a shithole – sorry Masha – for a whole month. I was, anyway. I was discharged because the magistrate described me as no more than a 'useful idiot' – his words – and I was deflated. Useful to whom? To the conspirators? To the authorities? Had I unwittingly betrayed something to a spy, in my cups? Anyway, no more cockroaches or rats for me; I didn't want my balls gnawed off. Sorry.

'But I was in an, er, ambivalous ... ambigalent ... situation, would ye call it? The other 'comrades' – ha! – remained in the rodents' dining-hall for a few more decades or for as long as they provided fresh meat. The lucky ones were taken to a forest and shot. Now what if there was still someone out there who was still pally with the comrades, or even with the cause, God blast it, and was gunning for me as a rotten old sneak – which I wasn't, Masha, I say again, not intentionally, but these junior officers were still hanging about in the stews where the students went, and I might ... have ... blurted out something that led a big-eared young fellow to promotion in the service of the His Imperial Majesty.

'Nobody was going to promote me to anything except some afterlife for disillusioned revolutionists, so I thinks, it's out of here, St Petersburg and all, back to Gavronzi, become good boy (within reason) down here in the sticks. So I meet your mother at a provincial ball. Pretty if pious. Good boy-hood of sorts established, manage the estate, faithful husband and all for a time at least.'

I ask him what happened to lady Russia. He empties his glass again, refills it.

'Oh, ah, the symbol, yes. She ... lady Russia ... doesn't wait for me. While I'm inside, she's fucking one of those worthy troops of the Tsar. Maybe the one who tipped off his high-ups about the Schiller-lovers and their poor benighted fellow-traveller yours truly. Look, Masha, that's it. I made an arse of myself once, but never again, y'know.'

I'm asking myself, then, and still now, what's his strength – now that I know his weakness? Will I ponder on all this in the future, and will it come to me some day at the end of a path in the woods? How am I like and unlike him?

[A few days later:]

An omen. Last night, I dreamed that I was gazing in my mirror, and saw myself with brushes and palette in one hand. Behind me, a harp. Well, then, I shall flourish in many arts! But the me in the mirror gazed back … she was pale, large-eyed, melancholy, as if only months from death.

Then she was lying in her coffin, the face and hands as white as her garments of death, as white as the coffin itself … I tried to look deep into the mausoleum, but it was dark behind her … I could pick up only a few details – crouched shapes as of two hooded women outside a sepulchre … the mausoleum itself suggested a large oriental kiosk.

In my sleep I was frightened but impressed with myself for my curious, perceptive eye - even in dream - for architectural detail. My smugness didn't last long into my waking hours, for this morning I took a sudden headache, missed my footing, the mirror slipped, fell, shattered … and there is now nothing but the kaleidoscope of my life before me.

And how should I interpret that?

How gather up the fragments into a new whole?

[That evening:]

Father suddenly announced that we were about to take a trip in the droshky. Just like that, not asking me or anything, a *fait* about to be *accompli*. I was initially annoyed at his presumption, then saw the smile on his face, and I smiled too … mind you, with reluctance. He was not to be allowed to assume that I would ever be in accord with him on the slightest matter.

I didn't mention Carignan – she was hardly going to be invited by either of us – but:

'What about Pavel?'

'Leave him. I've had enough of him, and his ways, over the past few days. Dammit, he's even Frenchier than you are. What a cissy. You, Masha, are no cissy.'

He thought he could get round me by such compliments.

I insisted that Paul – or rather Pavel: Father would never call him Paul even to Frenchify him – should accompany us. I strode into the music-room where Pavel was bashing away at an out-of-tune grand. (I preferred the modest instrument in my room.) When I told him about Father's planned expedition he hooted uncontrollably, without any of his usual finesse. Pavel prefers wit to belly-laughter … so why this behaviour?

He refused to explain and told me to go without him: ' – I … ah … have my own … ah! assignation later.'

He almost doubled up at that.

What was going on? My father yelled at old Sergei, his senile coachman, and after the shakiest ride I had ever known, the droshky stopped at the village. We were going to church – what? We entered, not without trepidation on my part, in case the crooked cross dislodged itself from the dome and spilled my brains. Mindful, too, of the mirror's demise, I knelt down and laid my forehead on the floor. If you do this three times on your first visit to a church, your prayer will be answered.

(It was indeed the first time in that particular church: we would use a private chapel in the garden. One does not worship with the peasants.)

Father ignored the service.

Gospodin pomilul

'Up!' he commanded. I saw the dark, brown, uneven planks that served for steps and – my God! I obeyed him.

How could this seemingly small church contain so much? There were so many doors at the beginning of each flight of steps. I peered into one nook after another and saw candles – all these side chapels, here? I could hear murmuring. I expected to see a monk in each of these gloomy alcoves, akin to those underground cells, for holy hermits, in Kiev. Was I dreaming? We reached the belfry, and Father motioned me through a door to the outside parapet.

I was shaking with vertigo. My palms became moist. I was determined, though, that Father should not witness my fear. I recognised the layout of the village, the fields and forests beyond, partly familiar from my unwitting journey to the old prophetess Alyona.

Father motioned with his arm. 'This still belongs to me,' he growled. ''61 and the emancipitating ... emanci ... freeing of the serfs be damned. We have sixty servants in all at home, but if you asked any one of these creatures below and beyond, "who is your master?" they'd give you three names: Christ's, Tsar's, and mine. I'm glad to share 'em with such illustri ... exalted colleagues. By God, you can keep your Germans, your French, your English and Yankees with their mad machines – your peasant still has his Russian soul and won't sell it to any of these devils!'

Back in the belfry, and my fears are so mastered that I climb to the bells by means of a rickety ladder ... I'm minded to pull the bells, with all my strength, and I feel a great rush of power ... which in turn terrifies me again. My head is about to explode ... I

31

can't speak to my father, for it's like a nightmare and the words die on your lips ...

Kolokoli, kolokoli ...

I took my pad from my bag and sketched Sergei ... I became so absorbed that I lost my sense of time passing. Sergei didn't move; you could barely detect his breathing. Did he know he had become my model, and was he keeping still for his young mistress? Or was he talking to God?

His nose twitched and my reverie was broken. I replaced my artists' materials, tucked my bag into a corner of the vehicle, and ran into the tavern. It smelled of excrement and sweat, stale tobacco and vomited alcohol. I recognised the carbuncled station-master, as well as one or two villagers who had gawped at me on previous occasions. The station-master was far gone and with his cronies was setting our country to rights – 'Thrash the fookin Yids and save Rooshia!' And there was Father, red-faced and guffawing, with a blowsy woman on his lap, like Falstaff and his whore.

He fondled the creature all over. Underclothes heaved and rustled. As for her, she became raucous when she noticed me:

'Come here hen, cuddle yer Auntie Ivanka!'

Instead they cuddled each other. If, with these rheumy eyes, he was ever aware of my horror, he didn't let on ... at least until he howled in my direction:

'Here's my Holy Russia, my Joan of Arc!'

I fled, and instructed Sergei to take me home immediately; he could come back later for my father, if he was so minded.

7
Coda: A Raven of the Steppe

Marie took a last stroll through the park, taking the opportunity to savour any unexplored corners – or at least those forgotten since her childhood steps here so long ago, before she, mother and entourage migrated to Europe.

Her imminent departure had occasioned in her an unexpected (and welcome) mood of resignation, of serenity. The formal parterres and fountains had been reasonably well-tended by the estate's gardeners. Not up to French standards, but no matter. She took pleasure in the relative symmetry of it all. The rose garden, the maze: Mozart after an excess of Beethoven or that new German they were talking about these days, in the west ... what had she read recently in a review: 'preferable the pipes of Papageno to the horns of Valhalla'?

As she walked further, though, there were increasing signs of neglect. She came to a thicket within which she detected the hint of a path. She parted the branches before her, and her persistence was rewarded. The path took a slight incline upwards and through the leaves she saw what appeared to be white columns.

The thicket gave way to a grassy clearing and she was cheered by the light flooding around her. She could make out distant hills and forests. It was her final Russian panorama.

The columns belonged to a square temple, incongruously Hellenistic, atop a mound. She had taken the gentler route, from the back, for before her a long flight of steps descended in stages from the temple to the grounds far below. Down there, an artificial lake looked stagnant, and contrasted bizarrely with a real one stretching just beyond the boundary of the estate. Autumn was approaching, and the trees which occasionally flanked the steps, thickening as they reached the level of the lake, carried a tinge of gold. She could picture the scene in a month's time: glorious but subdued, the sunset rendering pink these Ionic pillars, the steps, and the little urns perched at regular intervals on either side of the descent.

There were hints of mellower times to come. It had been raining and while the temple's floor was well protected – it may have been a folly, but it did function, after all, as a shelter – the classical predictability of the steps was offset by puddles whose presence seemed almost an impudence. Untamed nature getting its revenge on this man-made landscape.

The sky over these blue hills seemed to Marie to demand that she brood with it, in solidarity with a terrain striving to be free. She knew that her skill was not yet ready to capture this on paper, let alone canvas. The recognition both saddened and exhilarated her. Impatience was to be endured, but challenge was to be relished. She would return some day, long into the future perhaps, but assuredly; first, she must submit herself to new, self-chosen rigours.

Why I am not that raven of the steppe
Cawing defiantly there above me?
I would fly to the fogs of the far west,
The castle's stones precipitous to the sea.
On my ancestral walls the proud shield,
The sword of my clan:
With but my wing I'd brush off the dust
For those stern splendours to be revealed.
From the minstrels' hall, I'd strum the harp
With these proud feathers; down and deep
Into the vaults, such music surely can
Call up the troubled knight from bitter sleep.
But my own dreams are idle. Alps and oceans
Bar all my claims: I breathe cold, alien air.
Why am I not a raven of the steppe?
Here was I born: my soul belongs elsewhere.
(After Lermontov)

8
L'Académie Rodolphe: A Flyting

'My God: what an image!'

'Thank you, dear master.'

'Och, come on Roddy, she's done better, yez both know that.'

'Ha! This is another dimension for her.'

'You are so sweet, master Rodolphe.'

'Och, Goad help uz.'

'I can't believe my eyes. My God!'

'Mmm ... I thrive on praise.'

'And I cannae believe my lugs.'

'Dear master, I love you. Can I call you by your first name? Dear lovely Julien.'

'Roddy pal, dinnae let her sweet-talk ye ... Och, I forget it, you startit it, ye wee toad ye.'

'Ha! Georgette darling, I am no toad, but a frog, and Marie here will turn me into a handsome prince.'

'Och away wi ye. Dae Ah huvtae listen tae this shite?'

'Marie dahling. Don't listen to Georgette. She's very charming in her rough way, but she's a philistine. A proletarian striving too hard to be a bourgeois, isn't it sad? But you, my dear, are a genius, you are my discovery. You came here from Russia, that land of all that is spiritually probing and tragically forgotten. Marie dahling, *you are making art history.*'

'She's makin a mess on the floor, so she is, wi other folk huvvin ti pick up her shawl and things when she draps them – Lady Muck! ... Marie, ye're no a bad lassie, but ye've got an awfy lot tae learn.'

'Yes, and I'll learn it all from our dear master.'

'No hen, I'll learn ye.'

'What are you talking about?'

'I meant, I'll teach ye. If ye're really serious aboot goin oot among the workin folk, "observin" them, like.'

'Yes, I shall be the Zola of the brush.'

'Awright fer you, hen. You'll can swing yer brush as much as ye like, whaur *you* are. But Ah've got tae find what space Ah can in here, same as maist folk ... stickin oor palettes intae each other's faces, stickin oor brushes intae each other's erses, and whit's he daein aboot it, eh? Pittin wee chalkmarks on the floor, so's tae mark oor territory, bi Goad!'

'Ladies, please! You are fighting like cats!'

'Ay, and what fir no? Territory! That's what cats needs. Ye come intae the arcade frae the street, and it smells o pish. Cats! Ay, ye come in, and it's even caulder than the street. By the time Ah'm through that nasty wee door, and I'm haulf-wey up the stair, windin and windin and makkin me dizzy, bi-Christ, Ah'm needin a pish.'

'Georgette, don't be so common.'

'Listen tae her. Then ye get tae the lavvy in here, that's the first thing ye've got tae dae afore ye can face yer easel, and ye see his papers aw stacked up! His bloody archive, he cries it! In the lavvy, fir Goad's sake! And there's mair o it behind cupboards and under tables. Ah'd wipe ma erse wi it, so Ah wud!'

'Ha! Listen to her, Marie. She would never do that because, deep down, she knows this is a sacred place – '

'Sacred my arse.'

'I indulge her, Marie. I love her. Not as much as I love you, of course, but I love her dearly. She is common, as you say, but so am I. Like her, I was born on the wrong side of the tracks. Little Julien Rodolphe from the Vaucluse. My father was a poor schoolmaster, as you know. Persecuted for his views. And his father? Ha, he never knew his father, never knew who his father was … Georgette, you too had a father in the shadows …'

'That's no quite the way I wud put it, but ay, I suppose.'

'Marie dahling, you are lucky. The Gods have given you great gifts. You knew your father, knew who he was … is?'

'Only too well …'

'Marie, Georgette, you must be patient. We shall turn this place around. You will all win prizes, I'll see to that. Then more students will enrol, students with money as well as talent. Americans, even. Then I shall open more Académies Rodolphe, throughout Paris! I – we – shall revolutionise the art education of women.'

'Hear him. His talk o money, filthy money, eh, Roddy! And revolution! The Third Republic's really pishin its breeks at that, so it is. And you such a great republican tae! That's why ye're wantin Americans, then – it's no their money, it's their republican principles. My arse it is.'

'My dahlings, my dahlings, I've got everything under control.'

'Here, Marie, here a minute, Two things. Two things, when Roddy says 'em, ye've got tae be really worried, ye've got tae be on yer guard. One is, when he says tae ye, "Dahling, can you do me a favour?" Two, when he says tae ye, "Dahling, I've got everything under control."'

'You may mock, you may mock.'

'Oh, Ah wull, darlin, Ah wull.'

'But you know this as well as I do: you know this as well as every student of poor little Rodolphe, me, of the Vaucluse: as well as every student of mine, past, present and to come.'

'Know whut?'

'That the passion for art, and one's dedication to art, are the only things that can make us love life. That nothing else across the universe is worth doing.'

'Och, I can think o a lot o other things, but they're no fir the ears o wee Marie here.'

'And another thing, you, I, and all my ladies know.'

'And what's that?'

That because of the work done here – by you all – the histories of art will need to be re-written.

9

The Académie Rodolphe: The Journal of Marie B.

March 1878

Almost six months have passed since I enrolled at the Académie
Rodolphe and now they want me to progress from drawing to –
painting! Ah … if six months is considered to be a short time, I must
be special. Do I myself, however, consider six months to be a short
time? Is thirty years of a life too short or too long to achieve what
one desires passionately to achieve? I shall die before I am thirty. I
know it. In my dreams I see three candles: that is our sign, where we
come from, of a death impending.

In any case, where we come from, women lose their beauty
after thirty. The new Russian writers are saying that, so I have
heard. They are all men, of course, but it is true; I don't need
Russian writers to tell me that.

Look at Louise Breslau – look at Louise Breslau, indeed!
How can one ignore Louise Breslau. She is years ahead of me and is
always winning first prize for this and that. But it is good to have
such a worthy rival. I do not wish to compete with mediocrities.

Work, fool, work, I tell myself, *from sunrise to sunset and –
if need be – beyond.* I must be the first student to arrive at the studio
and the last to leave. M. Rodolphe – Julien – spoke glowingly of me
to my mother:

'I thought at first she might be another spoiled young
aristocrat who would leave after a week because of the discipline –
and the frankness – on which we pride ourselves here. Madame,
your daughter is no dilettante. Far from it. She works like a
Protestant from the foggy north' – this with his smile and twinkle –
'and at the same time she possesses the vision of a holy woman of
the expansive east.'

He is not strong on tact, M. Rodolphe, but I think my
mother respects him, although she knows nothing about art and
cares less. I would hope she cares for her daughter …

To me he said, the other day:

'Dahling, they will try to hurt you, you know.'

'Who?'

'The modish critics – and the boring academics.' That was the cue for his conspiratorial grin: what a repertoire of facial expressions he has at his command.

Facial expressions! As for M. Tony, he is my teacher for most of the time, because Julien is too busy for me (even me) to monopolise him, the great Master. I sometimes think that facial expressions are all that Tony has. He can convey his meaning with the raising of an eyebrow or the curl of a lip. It's a delight to watch, even if it spells adverse criticism of some detail one hasn't quite got right.

He is of course quite vulgar, but so is everyone here, including little Julien, and except myself. He placed a sign in the toilet: DON'T JUST SIT THERE, THERE'S WORK TO BE DONE. He must be a Protestant from the foggy north. He is quite right. Not that one could possibly wish to sit for longer than is necessary.

Once he was peering at my work – it was a study of the (clothed) model, just a practice piece really.

'Did you do this?'

'Yes, M. Tony.'

'Mmmm.'

I waited anxiously for further clues.

'You've been with us how long?'

I told him.

'Mm.'

Silence for some minutes as he pokes his lovely head at various angles in front of my drawing.

'Nae bad – not bad. Not bad.'

That was his chief verbal sign. 'Not bad.' The words alone could mean anything, applause or blame. Sometimes he will expand just a little – 'Not bad, I suppose' or 'Not bad at all'. Is that damning with faint praise? Or praising with faint damnation?

It works anyway. He is an excellent teacher. He'll go off, abruptly, once he has guided me on my way, and then M. Rodolphe – Roddy – will appear, put his arm around my back, look at my work and say something like:

'Dahling, between us we shall slay the dragon of parochialism.'

No doubt. But I hear so little of that granite voice of M. Tony – who was, after all, the first to suggest that I could, maybe, probably, seriously, definitely, pick up a palette and face a canvas.

Surely, then, I must become an artist superior to those of my fellow-students who have been painting for months! People like Georgette, for example! I am very fond of that old crow – she's over thirty – but Roddy is right, she is abysmally common, and cannot be a serious contender on Parnassus.

I should begin with still life studies, simple ones to build up my confidence in handling a brush. Sound advice from myself to myself – but how to curb my impatience?

Still life. I saw it today, sure enough, in the Champs Elysées. Still death, more like. It was the most haunting tableau imaginable, for me at any rate, and I must capture it some day ... when I possess the necessary skill, and inclination.

I saw *him*, yes *him*, by himself, in a cab.

The Duke of H. He should have been standing masterfully on a crag, his plaid across his shoulder and his flanks. Instead, there he was, the head puffy and jowly, face entirely composed of grey, yellow, red blotches. Whiskers: suggestive of dried-up carrots.

The eyes were rheumy, full of a sentimental leer. The lips seemed to be touched up with a sickly pink dye, and between them the little teeth managed an irregular sonata of fake joy.

Now and then the familiar cigar would enter and exit that nasty aperture. The movement was mechanical, reminding me of these little mannequins which raise and lower their arms when you put a few sous into the machine at a railway station.

So the Duke of H. is a premature antique which will fetch nothing at auction. There's hope yet for my masterpieces-to-come!

I can't help thinking of a possible mask – we could fit it on to the skull of that skeleton we have in the studio, next to the out-of-tune piano which is played only by myself. I'd thumb out my own composition, *Marche funèbre pour un aristocrate écossais*.

How could I ever fall in love with any man? I'd always find something in him to laugh at. The lion's skin – but upon a donkey. Adonis unemployable except as a mountebank.

How am I writing this? He is of our class. The people at these soirées at the Russian embassy would be shocked. It is as well that our family are never invited, though my mother would insist on

40

my being there if we were. It would be a waste of my time better spent in the studio – but she could never understand the dedication of the artist. Actually, my mother would also be horrified at what I have just written about the Grand Duke of H.! I say, long live the Republic – of the Ukraine.

If she discovers this journal after my death, she'll tear out this page and fling it in the fire. I must be careful not to keep all my papers in the one place; I shall entrust the 'sensitive' material to sworn confidantes.

The Duke of H.?

The man's a pudding: I'll think no more of him.

May 1878

As I reach the old age of my youth, I'm attempting to clothe myself in indifference. It's my fate to be a creature of abrupt, zigzag changes … I think of the markings of a snake in the Jardin des Plantes, as it writhes to a point, then to a counterpoint – it's all in the patterns of the scales. It's more than externals, though, where I am concerned. All ups and downs, the pain of a lack of balance. This will sound too immodest even for me, but I am a female Faust, instructing Mephistopheles to enable her to embrace (simultaneously) the outermost reaches of the south and the north, the west and the east. Whatever these challenges, and the frenzies they provoke in me, they are preferable to the even tenour of most people's lives – the ninety-nine per cent with their perfect domestic and career arrangements. Among them, where will you find the fine, subtle gradations upon which creative work so depends?

Reader, you will say that I fancy myself to inhabit the realm where extremes meet. If only that were so. My troubles are precisely those extremes which *never* meet. That paralyses me, and I might as well join that ninety-nine per cent whom I profess to despise. If I could be really effectively at war with myself, the clashes would release energy, and I require energy above all else as I grow older and … *akh!* The other day I brought home a pile of bones from the anatomy class. At night, I contemplated them in the drawer of my dressing-table, and reflected that hidden within me is such a pile of bones …

I must look in the mirror, feel disgust at what I see, break the mirror (I'm good at that) and be galvanised for work that may destroy me. Fine, as long as my work outlives me. What I fear above all is that it won't outlive me because it won't exist.

August 1878

We are in Germany, in Bad Soden. I don't mind that it's full of Germans – I do mind that it's full of Russians. (Why did I consent to come here, to this land of sausages, with mother and her entourage? The time that I'll be wasting, it doesn't bear thinking about, so I'll change the subject).

It's not just the Duke of H.: hadn't Russia, too, failed me? Nothing can save my country, nothing.

I escape from the Kurhaus as much as I can, looking behind me, and take to the woods. How they criss-cross, zig-zag like the serpentine movements I was writing about – was that back in the spring? I try not to re-read this journal if I can possibly help it.

I breathe in the sharp, tingling perfume of the pines and evergreens. What a delight to come upon a little wooden hut, all cross-beamed, latticed with irregular logs, like a feature in one of the *Märchen*; I sit there, write a little, sketch a great deal more ...

After a rainfall I still venture here; the mud on my shoes doesn't bother me. A maid can clean them. How I made such a fuss above Spa, when I was obliged to negotiate the stepping-stones across a brook, for all the world as if I was negotiating my career as an artist, primly lifting my petticoats – akh! Spoiled child! After my unwelcome bath in a Russian lake, I'm a tough little lady, believe me.

I discovered two German expressions which perfectly evoke the benefits I receive from these walks. One is

Waldseligkeit

(roughly meaning, forest bliss)

and the other:

Waldeinsamkeit

(roughly meaning, forest alone-ness – mark, that, alone-ness rather than loneliness. Don't confuse that with the wet romantic idea of solitude ...)

As you can see, I prefer the second. When, reluctantly, I feel I should return to my tedious Russians (my mother has used a false name for us), I gaze longingly at a vanishing point in the woods – the point where the path seems to lose itself in a mass of ferns. Every time I see such a vanishing point, I tell myself that one day I should explore beyond it. At a late point in my artistic pilgrimage, I shall base a work on this notion ...

I played Liszt for hours this evening ... I was almost unable to stop, and afterwards my fingers ached. Is not the piano the veritable instrument of Faust, encompassing the full orchestra, and goaded by Mephistopheles?

Over the past few days we have been on an excursion through the little villages on the Rhine. I enjoyed the red wine they serve you in the inn at the top of the steep main street of Assmannshausen: it's so light that I didn't acquire my usual headache ... and I need to be well in case I feel the urge to do some work on the way ...

As indeed happened when our carriage arrived at the abbey church of the Maria Laach. This sacred place is the more impressive for its proximity to the lake, which fills a volcanic crater and describes an almost perfect circle. The twin-towered church is as large as our cathedrals, but presents an austere exterior. Inside it is more elaborate, but not nearly as much as our humblest chapels back home.

As for the human environment here, well! This is the land where the most ludicrous people in the world continue to celebrate their defeat of the most cultured people in the world. My pencil became fiercer as I caught a number of the visitors – plump Rhinelanders, dour Prussians as they smoked their pipes and drank their beer on the hotel terrace or by the kiosk. Mlle Carignan, whose authority fades with the passing of each hour, admonished me for my frivolity. Her presence these days is no more than symbolic; she has never been near the Académie Rodolphe – she could never face that.

I was in a mood for nature, Carignan or no Carignan, so we took the carriage along the road eastwards from the Abbey, ascending a gradual slope to the south of the lake. At the summit we found the perfect picnic spot, but before eating I had to put down the scene before me – the field unfolding serenely towards the lake, and the wooded hills in the distance on the north side. The midday sun

43

lit up the lake in an almost theatrical manner, and I wondered why they claim that blue is a cold colour.

We took our lunch on a flattish piece of ground between a volcanic mound and a small wood where, at its ferny corner, you could pick out a little *Bildstock* or wayside shrine: as always in these regions of the Roman church, it depicted the Madonna and child. When they were ready to put aside their labours, peasants would doff their caps here and kneel.

I sketched the shrine and explored the wood, to the consternation of la Carignan. It would be a small triangle of green on the map, but it was as deep and mysterious to me as if I had been in the middle of the Black Forest. Afterwards I skipped and danced on the summit of the mound, queen of the panorama of the rolling fields further to the south.

Suddenly I had a sense that I had been here before – *déjà vu*, as they say – a thrill of recognition that was followed by foreboding. There came to me a vague memory of childhood, of a time when we were hundreds of versts south of Poltava and beside the tumulus of our Bashkir ancestors. Against adult protests I had climbed it and played upon it. Horrified, I now clambered down from the German rock, begging Mademoiselle Carignan to reach inside the carriage and pass me the smelling salts.

I'll take whatever pleasures I can from life, but I won't dance lightly upon death.

10
An Appeal by Mme Hubertine Auric

Women of France!

Citizenesses!

That is not a word you have heard for a long time, as M. Victor Hugo would tell you. Citizens we have a-plenty. But we, the women, are the Pariahs of the Republic, and we must stand up.

We made common cause with the men in the struggle for our Republic, in the creation of our Republic, in the defence of our Republic. Had not the régime of the Parody Nephew made whores of both sexes? Beware, citizenesses, while you – we – push the cart, of those who leap inside for a ride. The opportunists flourished under Napoleon III, and they have flourished under MM. Thiers, MacMahon, Grévy, Ferry and even (despite our hopes of him) Gambetta.

We made common cause with the proletariat, as was fitting; most of our sisters suffer twice, as women and as proletarians. Now we must learn from the labour struggle and adapt its strategies – its passions – to our own. What can be more noble than this, that our sex nourishes those who will in turn nourish the starved and unsheltered?

Listen: I have met them, the starved and the unsheltered. They are not noble. Not yet. One day, I may well be forced to join them, for all my years of work for our cause, work not ill-paid or underpaid, but not paid at all. Can you sacrifice as I have sacrificed? Only my dear husband stands between me and destitution. Like the rest of you, I am a dependant.

Join me, women of France. Join me, my citizenesses. What are your talents? Tell me, and I will find you tasks to match them. Can you portray our country as it is, not the lies that gather under chandeliers, but the rotting heaps behind the railings and below the steps? As a great Englishman has written: *It is the vainest of affectations to try to put beauty into shadows, while all the real things that cast them are left in deformity and pain.*

11
L'Académie Rodolphe

'Georgette, we must respond.'

'She's a gallus wumman, Ah'll gie her that.'

'We must do more than praise her, Georgette. We must join her.'

'Marie darlin. Whit's goat intae ye? Ye wis a stuck-up wee bitch when ye jyned this schuil. Nou ye're talkin aboot supportin tinks like me. The liberation o the proalytare-i-at an aw that pish. Christ, hen, yez are aw the same. Talk like a bluddy book.'

'Georgette: I am a Republican. Yes, you heard me talking my adolescent nonsense about the Prince Imperial, poor man. I could have been a fine Empress for him.'

'Ay, if ye'd been a Bonapartist, an ye probably wis!'

'Now he's gone. A spear through the heart, they say, when he was fighting the Zulus for the English. These English ... they are traitors, and with their stupid Queen too. So I cannot be a monarchist, can I? I wish Hubertine had not quoted an Englishman, though his words have stirred me. I prefer the Irish, who are now fighting for their freedom, probably also the Scotch ...'

'Marie hen, will ye stoap bummin on? Ah don't know nuthin aboot Zulus, an Irish, Scoatch, and bluddy affectations and byootiful shadows an aw that. Ah juist get oan wi ma life, daein what Ah'm best at.'

'But we women could get a chance to do better at what we're good at. If we band together. Listen: I'm free of that tiresome old witch Carignan. At last they've decided I'm old enough to explore darkest Paris.'

'Huh! You dinnae know nuthin aboot darkest Paris. Paris isnae a handsome stranger, right? Well, a stranger, that's sure, tae you onywey.'

'You know Paris.'

'Ay, hen, like Helen o Troy ... See, Marie, Ah'm a reader. Ah'm no entirely pig-iggorant.'

'You know Paris. Then show me it. But first of all come with me to Hubertine's meeting.'

'Tak yer Carignan alang wi ye. She'll shite her knickers, lissenin tae aw that.'

46

'Oh my God! What an image! Seriously, though, Georgette, I'm free now, to go about alone, to sit on the benches in the Tuileries, in the Luxembourg, to visit the artists' shops, the churches, the museums, without some ancient harpie behind me, reporting everything back. The younger girls here don't have that. How can their art possibly have a chance to develop?'

'Ay, ay. But whit ye're gettin at is, ye're no completely free.'

'Ye ... es. You're right, I can do all these things. They're no more or less than what any mature bourgeoise can do. But I'm not free to ... to amble about the Latin Quarter, to walk these old streets at night ...'

'Ye could if ye were a hüre. And yer Hubertine says that yer Napoleon made us aw hüres.'

'Be serious. To trace the Parisian labyrinth ...'

'Goad give me strength!'

'To trace ... the labyrinth. That's the freedom you need. Otherwise you can never become a true artist.'

'Wuid ye lissen tae her!'

'Georgette, please. Come with me to Hubertine's. She's a wise woman ... You're a wise woman. Educate me, help me to mature.'

'Och, aw right then, Ah'll be yer chaperone.'

'No, Georgette, I'll be yours.'

'Ye've goat a wey o persuadin folk. Ah'll gie ye that. But hear me, Marie. Ah'm no wantin tae lissen wan bluddy evenin efter anither tae a loady toffs talkin shite.'

'Honestly, Georgette. Show some appreciation. Hubertine and her comrades want to save your people, your class.'

'That's juist the problem, hen.'

12
Rue Cail, 21

The clerk peered suspiciously from the grille of his kiosk, took their francs, slapped down their tickets on the green-matted counter.

'Very daring,' said one of the passengers. 'Look, a poster for a new novel by M. Zola.'

The other passenger stared at the advertisement and hunched her shoulders.

'You're not saying very much,' said the first. 'You're not saying anything. Yet here we are, the sight and the sound of Paris today – the wrought-iron and glass, the clatter of new carriages. How can we take all this for granted?'

The other kept looking around, as if to check they weren't being followed. They boarded, and after three stops they found themselves at the end of an ill-lit lane to the north of the Gare de l'Est.

No. 21 – here it was.

A slight woman in her mid-thirties answered the door, holding it slightly ajar. Her ample hair was unkempt, rope-like in its twists and rough ends; her clothes, though old, emitted a musty rather than an acrid smell.

The visitors asked for the mistress of the house.

'That is me,' replied the woman. The voice was formal, 'educated', thought the visitors to themselves. They made a sign.

The woman looked at them, and apparently judging that they could be trusted, opened the door more widely and allowed them in. They ascended, led by one or two weak futters of gaslight. The salon – if it could be so called – was occupied by a motley of rugs, papers and books.

'I am Pauline,' said the first visitor.

The second visitor said nothing.

'She is with us,' said the first. 'But just a little shy.' The second grinned ironically. The first offered a little modification. 'Apprehensive.'

'Apprehensive,' repeated the lady of Rue Cail, no. 21. 'Very sensible. The new freedoms – they can be taken away at any time. But we must speak out. Honour demands it. Yes, honour. The men have besmirched that word. We must reclaim it.'

48

'The cause demands no less. Whatever M. Zola can get away with, so should we.'

The lady of no. 21 scrutinised Pauline.

'So, Pauline. You're a writer.'

'And ... more, as I told you in my letter. My friend here is also that "more", but she is too cautious.'

'Sympa?'

'Of course, or she wouldn't be with me.'

'Perhaps we can persuade her to contribute.'

'We'd need to persuade her to talk first.'

'Yes, because otherwise, and in due course, the police would persuade her.'

The second did not grin this time, but looked around sharply on hearing a scratching noise.

'Mice,' said no. 21.

'We are tigresses,' remarked Pauline, 'pursued by mice.'

No. 21 allowed herself to smile.

'Pauline. I must tell you straightaway. There is no money in this. If you write for us, it is for the cause. It is part of your commitment.'

Pauline's expression answered this frankness in like manner.

'It is not a bourgeois paper,' said no. 21.

'I am not a bourgeoise,' said Pauline.

'Yes, I can hear that,' remarked no. 21, again with that smile, forced as it was.

'And neither is my friend.'

Pauline's friend said nothing to prove or disprove this. 'It is the language of the body,' said no. 21. 'Not the language of the lips. The language of the body, that is what reveals the class ...'

'Of those who don't use their lips,' smiled Pauline, gesturing at her friend.

'Alas,' sighed no. 21. 'Most women use their lips, but not to speak.'

...

'Well?'

The visitors were on their return journey.

'Yer Hubertine? She's awright, Ah s'pose,' said Georgette. 'But aw that high and mighty way o talkin! Ah cannae be daein wi

49

it, Mademoiselle Pauline.' She uttered the name with her old grin. 'Sorry, *Citizeness* Pauline.'

'In order to do anything in this world,' said Citizeness Pauline, 'we have to put up with a little ritual now and then. Especially where I come from.'

'Whitever that means. Look, Marie, Ah'll stick tae picters. If you wantae branch oot intae this, guid luck tae ye. No aw o us has that luxury.'

'That's cruel, Georgette,' said Marie. 'I'll pretend you weren't being serious.'

'Ay, and maist o us can stick anely tae juist the wan name. Marie, Pauline, wha are ye goannae be nixt? Joan o bluddy Arc?'

'How about Marianne?' smiled Marie. 'After all, Hubertine wants to rescue the Republic.'

'Marianne, eh?' snorted Georgette. 'Ah cannae see you as a revolutionary sans-culotte, hen.'

'Well, maybe it's revolutionary to be as versatile as I am.'

A man lurched out of a drinking den, just in front of them.

'Yukh! There's yer bluddy proles fir ye, Marie. Save him if ye can.'

Ah belong tae Paaa-rish
Dear auld Paris toun

'Lissen tae that. Bet ye didnae see sights like him doun Nice way. Hey, pal, ye're nae fukkan nightingale. Sorry, Marie. But he's juist an auld craw o the night, the puir bugger.'

And when Ah've a drink o a Saturday night,
Paris belongs tae me!

'Does it hell. He's kiddin himsel!'

'I agree with you there, Georgette.'

'Nor should it belong tae him.'

They reached the Père-Lachaise Cemetery, entered it.

'That's whaur they shot the Communards. Lined them up against the waw, bang, bang, bang, that wis it. Tit fir tat. Efter aw, the Communards had cut up their lot, even the odd Archbishop. But that's the wey o the world, Marie. Eye fir an eye, tooth fir a tooth. The Communards meant well, Ah'll gie them that, but they cuid haurdly expect mercy. Ah'm no wan fir martyrs, Marie.'

Georgette stared hard at her friend.

'You werenae here in eichteen-seeventy. Did Ah no hear you say that you and yer mammy and her flunkies aw buggered aff tae the bright lights o Geneva? Eh? Well, Ah'll tell ye, doll. It wis bad enough wi the bluddy Pruscos. If they didnae stick ye wi their bayonets, they'd dae it wi the spikes on their helmets. Us women said it wis mebbe cos their cocks wisnae lang enough. Sorry, Marie. The Communards were supposed tae be on the side o the folk, and shair enough, they probly wis. Workin folk theirsels, mony o them. But things juist got worse and worse. Ah'll tell ye, hen, if ye huvnae had tae survive on rat soup and cat stew, ye must've lived an awfy sheltered life.'

Marie wasn't listening. She was pointing out a mausoleum – a bombastic affair, but with its own quirky exoticism that made it all the more hilariously pompous.

'I'd like to end up in something like that,' said Marie, brightly.

'Ye're welcome tae it, hen. If ye can afford it.'

'But not yet. I've got too much to do first.'

'Then juist stick tae the wan thing, hen, and ye'll get the grave o yer dreams.'

13
L'Académie Rodolphe

'For you, Marie dahling, it is the order of release. These younger ones, with their tedious interfering mothers, we must keep ... back until they are ... ready to become mature artists. Some that you have left behind are older than you, but they too have tedious, interfering mothers ...'

'I am strong, M. Rodolphe. Stronger than my mother. She realised that when she dismissed Mlle. Carignan, who is probably now persecuting some young bourgeoise lacking in determination. I have reached my *Wendung*.'

'Your – what?'

'My *Wendung*. My turning-point. It's German.'

'Ah, Germans. The people who prefer their beer and sausages to art. Did you know that during the war they used M. Pissarro's canvases as duckboards? They tramped their boots over masterpieces.'

'I know nothing of M. Pissarro.'

'You will.'

'I am not interested in these people of impressions, of mere evanescences. I shall paint what is solid and lasting.'

'Ah, my dear Marie, we are arguing when we should be celebrating. I just hope that your *Wend* – your turning-point – will not swirl you further in the direction of M. Zola. He is a good man, I must concede that with all my heart, and he so eloquently defended M. Manet and his colleagues, but ...'

'You're going to say that he's a "mere writer".'

'Why, yes, dahling. They cannot understand our art, it is higher than theirs. Indeed I would dispute that literature is an art at all. The image is subtle, the word is obvious. It's everybody's currency.'

'Everybody's? And that's wrong? I thought you were a Republican? For the people?'

'Yes, yes, I am a man for the future. I belong to the South, you know, and we are people of purpose. But we are also people of faith as well as of reason. Reason can take us only so far. The Positivists fail to realise that. It is faith which enables us to transcend reason ...'

'And also transcend reality? Is that healthy, M. Rodolphe?'

'Ah, Marie dahling, I allow you to graduate as a full artist ...'

'Yes, Julien, my dear, dear, master. You give me my freedom and I respond so ungratefully by doing what I like.'

'You are so cruel. But you are so beautiful. Cruelty always accompanies beauty. My dear, you are in danger of becoming a realist, a realist of the new sort – what is it, a naturalist – that is M. Zola's tedious term. His prefaces and articles have become so boring. It is all *derrière-garde*, if I may say so: M. Tony's phrase, ha! a good one too. Some of you would-be revolutionaries are actually conservatives in disguise.'

'M. Tony! I bet he used that phrase to describe *my* work, but you won't say ...'

'Now, M. Courbet, another good man, indeed a great man, greater than M. Zola but of course painters are always greater than writers ... M. Courbet thinks of himself as the great revolutionary, the socialist ... yes, he was imprisoned for his beliefs, and that is courage which I can admire. But when a country priest, a simple, humble, devout man, requested M. Courbet to paint an angel in his church – do you know what M. Courbet said?'

'Yes, yes, M. Julien. You've told us before ...'

'M. Courbet said to the priest, this good little man without pretensions, he said to him: "Show me an angel and I'll paint you one!" Oh yes, he had to make his clever realist point to the poor priest who only wanted to bring a little joy into the villagers' place of worship. It was crass. It was insensitive. That from a man who professes to be for the people! He despises the peasants ...'

'He didn't despise the stonebreakers.'

'No, and his "Stonebreakers" is a masterpiece, one of the glories of French art. But realism – beware of it when it becomes a dogma! It glorifies all that is mechanical, all that is superficial – mere photography! Yes, I do blame the camera, it's a terrible invention.'

'Now who is *derrière-garde*!'

'Faith, faith! Not reason and photography, but – imagination. That divine faculty, as M. Baudelaire has so eloquently put it. Imagination.'

'You're quoting a "mere" writer.'

53

'M. Baudelaire was a poet, and a profound Catholic who would not fashionably deny the existence of sin. He understood our art, too, better than M. Zola. For M. Baudelaire – God rest his troubled soul! – a great piece of art criticism could be undertaken within a sonnet, rather than in an interminable academic, scientific treatise. Marie dahling, I love you, you have it within you to achieve greatness, but flee, I beg you, the heresy of realism. It is the aesthetic of the bourgeois ...'

'You take the bourgeois's money, especially when he's American. All these dollar-worshippers who are enrolled here. You know they are without talent.'

' ...and it is the aesthetic, equally, of the socialist. They are materialists both. As M. Flaubert so eloquently expresses it: "The cult of the stomach breeds wind."'

'Another writer!'

'They may aspire to art, even if they don't achieve it as we do. We must admire their heroism.'

'It sounds like you are being very condescending to the writers, M. Rodolphe. For all you know, I may be one of them.'

14
From *La Citoyenne*, March ---, 1881

… Women are admitted to the State Medical School; why not to the State Art School? A mystery. Perhaps the feminine element would prove a source of scandal in such a legendary centre of alternate boredom and intrigue. Yet we have only to follow the example of the Schools of Stockholm and St Petersburg – yes, even St Petersburg is more liberal towards women artists than the Paris School! In Sweden and Russia, even though the studios with live models are kept separate from the rest, all students can be reunited for the plenary classes.

But the question of segregated or mixed classes is of less importance than the fact that, here in Paris, women are barred from the State School altogether.

Gentlemen (if gentlemen you are), you who bellowingly proclaim yourselves stronger than us, more intelligent, more gifted than us, you still feel that you have to jealously and nervously guard, for yourselves alone, one of the finest schools in the world where you receive every advantage. If we are so inferior, what are you afraid of?

Those women whom you claim to be frail, weak, limited, and of whom a great number are forbidden even the banal freedom to come and go as they please, by order of that word 'propriety' – you, gentlemen, offer them neither encouragement or protection. You deny them even the honour of patronising them.

Not all women are going to become artists, just as not all want to become legislators. We are talking about a very small number of women. You know that well enough.

We have enough design schools in the city for those who will serve industry, but not enough schools for those who wish above all to serve art. At the most we have two or three studios for young rich women to play at being painters.

What we need is to be able to work as men do, and not be obliged to play circus tricks in order to obtain what men enjoy as a matter of course.

We're asked with indulgent irony: how many great women artists have there been? Ah, sirs, you'd be amazed at how many there have been, given the enormous difficulties they have encountered.

Let us now speak to people about how they need to send their daughters to draw from the nude without which they cannot study properly. These people think nothing about taking these same daughters to the beaches of Trouville and Dieppe, where male flesh is amply – too amply – on display. It is absurd that there is no protest when women freely observe paintings of the nude, while it is forbidden to them to make their own drawings from live models.

As for the women who are too poor to indulge in such delicacy, they don't have the benefit of an education, refused as it is by the State.

Women are prevented from studying at all by means of intricate Gothic procedures; they are denied access to courses in anatomy, perspective, aesthetics, etc., that men simply take for granted.

Women are not admitted to the competition for the Prix de Rome. They're not even permitted to prove the 'incapacity' which you claim for them.

Fortunately certain annual exhibitions are open to us and the recent salons have demonstrated that there are those of our disdained sex who are conscientious and industrious, holding high the banner of the free school, the Atelier Rodolphe, which has opened its doors to them. It could go further, though, and use its prestige to echo our appeal: *it is not by depriving women of the means of satisfying a noble passion that they will be inspired with a desire to spin wool.*

Pauline MORELL.

15
The Journal of Marie B.

March --, 1881

The Tsar has been assassinated. I have learned some of the details from reading the French journals and from hushed conversations with certain obscure Russian exiles here in Paris.

He was returning to the Winter Palace after inspecting a parade. It happened in a quiet street along a canal; bombs were thrown. He managed to whisper to his brother, 'Take me home to die.' He was escorted on his sledge by Cossacks – from our part of the country – on horseback; they themselves must have been a fearsome sight, dark angels spattered with blood. The Tsaritsa had anticipated that she and her husband would be taking their Sunday afternoon stroll in the Summer Gardens.

The tragic death of the Tsar makes me weep. His successor, Alexander III, is supposed to be very liberal, but so are they all when they come to power. The murdered Tsar freed the serfs in '61, and my father – for all his own early liberalism! – was not excited about that. It is said that when Alexander II was killed he had the plans for a Russian Parliament in his pocket. When one thinks of the horrors of which Russia used to sup full, the 'insolence of office' as Shakespeare would call it … it would be excellent if this new Tsar would give the country a Parliament.

What an example that would be! Long live the universal Republic!

May ---, 1881

The leader of the Tsar's assassins was a woman. I am half in sympathy [the MS. at this point is heavily crossed out.] A great uprising will not be easy to achieve … Just now there will be killing of Jews or at least smashing of their houses. There is much of this talk in the cluttered offices of *La Citoyenne* at Rue Cail, 21. There are people here who are fearful for their relations back home.

The new Tsar remains in his stupid inertia … He didn't have to be afraid of giving in to threats by giving us liberty! He had only to attribute such an enlightened policy to his father, saying: 'You've killed him at the moment when he was going to reform the Empire. In giving you liberty, I'm only fulfilling his last wish.'

Everything would have been saved. Does he think that he'll be able to perpetuate the autocracy?

Akh! My poor country!

16
L'Académie Rodolphe

'Mademoiselle Marie: I'm astonished.'

'Astonished! But M. Tony, you always said I had it in me.'

'Yes, yes ... the technique. Nae doot ... no doubt about that. True, it was, still is, affa ... awful *derrière garde* ... I'm talking too much.'

'Which would be unusual for you, M. Tony.'

'What I mean is ... the subject matter. Not yours, I'd have thought, to put it mildly. But I recognise all this ... it's uncanny. I was a bit loun ... wee boy like these young fellas there. Yes, him on the right with his chin thrust out. Almost as if you'd been staring at me and ... imagined me at the age of ten. You've been staring at me, haven't you? Fit an affa quine ye are ...'

'Me? Staring at you, M. Tony? You must think I'm a terrible coquette. Maybe I am.'

'You could stare at a lot worse than me.'

'Oh, I've no doubt about that, M. Tony. And at a lot better. But you're an attractive man, quite dapper in your way. A good woman could work on you. Improve on you, a few touches here and there and oolalah! She'd create a masterpiece out of you, M. Tony.'

'Perhaps you've done that already, here, Mademoiselle Marie. But I've got competition, it seems. These other boys are also there, to the life. The stance o thon big lounie at the left ... he's the high heid-yin, fit's he showin them? They're up tae nae good, Mademoiselle Marie. I wis up tae nae good at that age, until wee Roddy rescued me. If I wasna here I would be in a jyle richt nou.'

'My, you are loquacious today, M. Tony ... dear Tony.'

'And there ye are yersel at the richt o the picture, walkin like a richt proper wee miss, awa frae them. Ye're scunnert wi their ploys ... ye're turnin awa frae their wee lounie conspiracies, frae thon rickety fence that marks their territory ...'

'So you think the little girl is me, eh, M. Tony? Maybe yes, maybe no. And she'll be off to write a piece for *La Citoyenne*, eh? Against the little boys of the Salon who stick only their own daubs on the fence, and tear off everybody else's?'

'Ah, Marie, now you shouldna ... shouldn't be standing there, writing in your own head an interpretation of your own painting.'

'Why not?'

'That's my job.'

'That's me told, then.'

'And the title o the thing – "Le Meeting" – why d'ye use an English word? Is that necessary?'

'Yes, like the painting itself, it's about doing what hasn't been done before.'

'Is that so. Well, it canna be completely original, I'll tell ye that.'

'How so?'

'That tozie hüre – fit d'ye cry her – Georgette must have taken ye there, wherever it is ... though I've a bittie o an idea that I ken faraboots it is ... whereabouts, likes. Ye shouldna go there on yer ain, that's certain, but she shouldna hae taen ye there.'

'Maybe I did go there on my own, M. Tony. Georgette's not my chaperone. I had enough of my chaperones in my ... youth.'

'She's yer mentor, then.'

'Excuse me?'

'She's giving you something anyway, an insight you wouldn't ever obtain on your own, and you want that to separate you from the other ladies in this school.'

'Please elaborate.'

'I dinna need tae. You're jealous o the students here that are as good as you, forby better ... No, mebbe I shouldna hae said that, true or not.'

'Oh Tony, dear Tony, I'm not that thin-skinned. There's nothing like a rival to spur one on.'

'Ay ... right ... don't I know it, like these bit lounies there. But mebbe yer true mentor isn't here at the Academy Roddy. Mebbe the rival spurrin ye on isna here either.'

'What! None of these Swedes and Poles with their studied soulfulness, always out to impress you and M. Rodolphe? These foreigners who think they're so intellectual and profound and are merely sheltered bourgeoises who think they can fool you by playing the charismatic exotic?'

'Isn't that what you are, Marie?'

'Ha, ha! You've exposed me, dear old Tony. Maybe there's a little bit of truth in your accusation. Oh! It doesn't make me want to slap your face: it makes me want to cuddle you.'

'Well ... I'm wrong about the bourgeoise ... and you're not sheltered, at least not if you can paint stuff like this. But you are exotic.'

'Nonsense. I'm as French as you are. Dear lovely Tony! Ah! But who is this mentor of whom thou speakest? Speak now, name the wretch, or I cut off thy comely head. No, I will cut off her head instead.'

'His head.'

'A man? It's not you, is it?'

'No.'

'Then who? What is his nationality? Swedish? Polish? My God, not American?'

'No, French ... as French as you are ... but more so. In fact, he's somebody frae my pairt o France, a common mucky peasant like mysel.'

'Enough of these riddles –'

'It's Jules.'

'Jules, M. Tony?'

'Jules Bastien-Lepage.'

'My God ... Bastien-Lepage? *The* Bastien-Lepage? M. Tony, that's the greatest compliment you have ever ... Bastien-Lepage! To link my name to his! So he is my mentor, and not you or Georgette any more. He is my mentor, and I must follow him.'

'You can try, Mademoiselle Marie, you can try.'

'I beg your pardon?'

'He may follow you.'

17
The Journal of Marie B. : Le Meeting

May 3, 1884

I have arrived – after all these years. Still, I have much to learn, and so little time in which to learn it.

So far most of what I have learned can be traced, ultimately, to the example of Bastien-Lepage. But I need to 'go beyond' mere derivation. At twenty-six – according to my own plans made all these years ago – I should be the mature artist. ('All these years': there are those who will mock that phrase, I know that ...) I hear of imminent movements, as well as those already underway, which 'go beyond' realism. I was initially suspicious of what they called impressionism, and relished the jest that it was what M. Zola so bizarrely praised before he was given spectacles to correct his myopia. He had equated impressionism with realism because all that he could see in real life was a blur.

Perhaps now I shall paint impressionist pictures – or even dig out the ones I've already attempted. I keep them locked in a cupboard in my studio, and have shown them to no one.

Shall I show them to Bastien-Lepage, now that I have 'triumphed', now that I have met him?

I had avoided all opportunities to view this avatar in the flesh. I wanted to view only his work, not the man. No doubt I was jealous of him and feared that to meet him would intensify the feeling, that I'd be moved to assault him with my parasol or at least with a carefully aimed paintbrush.

Jealousy? I should have felt only gratitude!

Look at his Saint Joan. She has heard the voices, she has rushed forward, overturning her spinning-wheel, and stopped, leaning against a tree. Now that is how an artist should suggest movement – by fixing the moment just after the movement has taken place: the face upturned, having received the instant of illumination, the arm at the precise angle immediately following the action. .

I had arrived at the Salon, dreading that I would meet him. Do you know that I even avoided reading articles about him in the illustrated magazines, in case I saw an image of him – a photograph – no, an engraving, for that would have revealed more of his physiognomy than a photograph could have done. The most mediocre engraving, after all, may be touched by that divine faculty in which the camera – it's laughable to have to say this – must inevitably be wanting.

I look into my glass, and see not myself, but my perception of myself, a perception that may surprise and even shock me when I am made suddenly conscious of it.

I look into my glass, and see Bastien-Lepage, looming and fading, his features mingling momentarily with my own.

The jury's room was filled with pompous middle-aged men. At least Rodolphe and Tony, God bless them, had personality. (And Georgette, come to think of it.) I saw these two dear teachers of mine at the other end of the room, fidgeting. Were they anxious in case I would be successful and so never see them again, never again hear their encouraging words, never again share with them their pride in me? Akh, I have seen so little of them lately, and my intuition is that the hour of our parting is at hand.

You gave me so much, my friends, but you could not give me …

'Le Meeting' received an award – but not the medal which it deserved and which, as it turned out, the public demanded for it. Still, it was fêted with remarkable volubility by the stuffy professors, those generals in the army of art who condescend to the ranks. I bowed, was terribly shy … their enthusiasm turned to what appeared to be outrage … a woman, dammit, we've given a prize to a woman.

My God, suddenly they all appeared to resemble my father! I had to restrain myself from grabbing a pencil and any old piece of paper lying around – a leaf torn from their precious catalogue would have done nicely. A crowd of my fathers! In their murmurs I heard nervous confessions of the follies of their youth, their heroisms which had collapsed ignominiously into farce. I saw them divest their top hats and frock-coats, I saw their quivering nakedness, the folds of belly, the sweaty dangling genitals … I burst out laughing and fled from that grand room, that Salon which is supposed to be the space of aspiration for all good little artists!

No, they'd be saying, it can't be her. The woman's an impostor. Some raggle-taggle who's barged in from the streets. 'Not one of your bonbons, Jean-Christophe, eh?' – 'By gad, sir, in the good old days I'd have demanded satisfaction for that remark.' – 'Only joking old chap, but she's deuced pretty, I'll say that.'

I darted past such mediocrity there – that absurd pastry-shop 'Gloppe' thing by M. Béraud, with the so-nice ladies delicately nibbling their slices at round tables, the round-backed chairs so delicately sat upon, not unlike the round-backed chairs in the Ostend Kursaal, the round-backed chairs that I rocked and tilted myself upon, causing all manner of minor scandal … It all came back: that was the summer when I was determined not to become a young lady …

I didn't dart past the masterpieces of Bastien-Lepage.

But hurry, I must escape - this door, God, it's heavy … ah, here's a courtyard, with potted plants. A poor tree, straggling, struggling, striving to assert itself, surrounded by a veritable palace of lifelessness – Bastien-Lepage apart, of course, and … my 'Le Meeting'.

I plomped down on a … round-backed chair, sighed with relief as I struck my fists on a … round table, laughing to myself as it occurred to me that I was recreating the 'Gloppe', but with my own unique energies … and I screamed when I saw the legs of another person, a man, at the courtyard's only other little round table, hidden by a luxuriant palm and a newspaper which he was pretending to read …

'Ah, you, too are hiding, Monsieur.'

Nervously he rustled his newspaper, realised he must put it aside and answer me if he was any sort of gentleman.

(Oh, that poor straggling, struggling, striving tree … that single tree, no forest here, no hope here of *Waldseligkeit*.

But not alone: no *Waldeinsamkeit* either …)

'No, no, Mademoiselle … I wisna … I was not … hiding. I apologise, Mademoiselle. I wis … was lookin for the exit, and I couldna … could not find it.'

He sounded like Tony, and yet not so.

I must take a closer look at him, but he seemed unable to emerge from that dark corner behind the palm.

'I was looking for the exit myself. We could find it together, Monsieur.'

'I will go ahead, Mademoiselle, and try to lead you to the exit.'

64

'Ladies first, Monsieur. I shall find it first, and you may graciously come after.' I was embarrassing the poor devil.

When he emerged from behind the palm, I felt guilty at my raillery. He was small, with a round face, not unbecoming but not especially becoming either. The hair was neatly cut – is this, I thought, what one of their country priests looks like? The moustache was wispy, and I wondered if he were capable of growing a beard. But what eyes, the darkness there that could both absorb and radiate an uncanny light …

The voice was piping – I have said that I was reminded of Tony, but that was the accent. He had nothing of Tony's rough baritone, though his own voice was rough enough. His jacket, which was faded, lent him a weird blend of absurdity and dignity. All the buttons were fastened. He bowed, clumsily enough, but not without a certain naïve charm. I knew that I must not hurt this man for all the world.

He must have been struggling valiantly with his shyness, for he came right out with:

'You are the artist of "Le Meeting", Mademoiselle.'

'Yes … I am … I am sorry for my performance in there …' I shut up, because I realised he couldn't have been at the scene in the jury room. I'd have noticed him, even in that crowd.

'They thought the work was by a man.'

Well! This was becoming more interesting by the minute.

'Did they now, Monsieur.' I regretted my tone, but he was becoming bolder, and I couldn't help admiring him for it.

'I heard them say … fa … who is this Monsieur Bashkirtseff? Strong stuff, they said, this Monsieur Bashkirtseff paints strong stuff.'

I had signed it M. Bashkirtseff; they had clearly taken the 'M.' of 'Marie' to be 'Monsieur'.

Then the little man before me, the bashful bumpkin in his tight-fitting jacket, really astonished me.

'It's by a lady, I told them. No, they said, it's by you, Monsieur, it's your style – the impudent brats of the gutter, they said, you go in for that sort of thing, Monsieur. I replied that, unlike the artist of "Le Meeting", I dinna … don't know the poor of the city, I know only the poor of the villages and the ferms … farms. They said, come, come, Monsieur, don't give us that, "Le Meeting" is by your good self, Monsieur, but what an outlandish name you

65

chose to sign it with, you are playing tricks, Monsieur … that's what they said to me … but I humbly apologise, Mademoiselle, I should not be blethering like this, I'm very sorry.'

'No, no, this so funny … these old fellows addressed you as Monsieur … but Monsieur who? Since you are clearly not Monsieur Bashkirtseff.'

I enjoyed that thrust.

'Monsieur Jules B… '

'Ah! Another Monsieur B.!'

'I'm Bastien-Lepage.'

…

When I had recovered, I started to laugh. I shouldn't have done that, but my emotions were veering off in all directions.

'Well, Monsieur Jules Bastien-Lepage: my pleasure. And I have to confess to you that I am indeed Monsieur Bashkirtseff.'

He doesn't know how to take me, this poor soul. I must behave myself.

Only I didn't.

'But I don't like the French form of my name.'

I shouldn't have said that, for he began to stammer: he believed that he had offended me. I must make all well, or he would rush from this courtyard, make for the exit, and I'd never see him again.

'Bashkirtseva. Mariya Konstantinovna Bashkirtseva. It's a proud name, a stirring name, but jerky and fretful. Oh dear, Monsieur, I am not very French after all.'

'Mademoiselle, perhaps it is possible … sometimes … to be …too French.'

I could see we were going to get on very well. He was speaking a language that was not his own, it was too refined for him, and yet now and then there would emerge a quiet elegance that didn't sound in the least pretentious. I couldn't resist one riddle for him:

'The mystery remains however, Monsieur. How could they think "Le Meeting" was by you, when it was signed by that elusive Monsieur Bashkirtseff? Have you been using my name, you rogue, and have I been using yours?'

He didn't laugh at this. I didn't expect him to laugh. But he was not offended. The poor dear could not possibly be offended by anything that I or anyone else might say. He merely blushed!

(Yes, we shall get on very well indeed.)

So he allowed me to approach the exit first - and he manfully followed.

18
Memo from one of the Gentlemen of the
Salon to a Close Friend and Colleague

I understand that the fellow Rodolphe has patched things up with us anent the behaviour of Mademoiselle Bashkirtseff at the awards ceremony. He said it was 'women's trouble, that kind of thing.' Well, be that as it may. It was made clear to Rodolphe that because she was one of his, it would be hushed up as much as it can be. We can certainly lean on the journalists who were there etc. etc., but I tell you, in all confidence, that no matter how talented she was, if she were my daughter, I'd have her horse-whipped.

If only we'd known the damn thing was by a woman ...

19
Travail à Deux

'Who shall dare to say that a potato is inferior to a
pomegranate?'
JEAN-FRANÇOIS MILLET
(1814-75), painter of peasant life.

Jules and Marie ... and the long island in the river,
The frontier of field and street, of Jules and Marie,
Where they – and their subjects – meet of an afternoon,
The Grande Jatte: what's flow and fixity forever
Though blended strokes may yield to neighbouring dots,
And what was whole, fragment: Monsieur Seurat
One day in June, unrecognising, glances,
Smiles, at our sketching couple: *dalliances,*
No doubt, of such and such who frequent idly
This fine observable spot. But Jules and Marie?

Marie and Jules. She records a squat bourgeois
With rubicund grin, sharp beard, dancing his Sunday
Jig before his siren. Jules, for his part,
Draws a bored boy, with tethered horse and cart,
Leaning against a post, through acrid smoke
Laughing into himself at these posh folk.
Marie takes in the well-attired array
Of all the classes: subtle panorama,
Dowager or flower-girl under an ample hat.
- Students, Marie and Jules, of the Grande Jatte.

Jules and Marie: here, in this neutral space,
At last he's free from the city of formulas.
The damp bundles of letters in wooden frames,
His youth crying for the voices in his dreams,
The infantryman ranked to defend the heights
Of the suburbs: when a Prussian bullet cuts
Him down, and he sees out the war in clinics
Safe at least from attacks by Salon critics.

69

Now he lays by past clerking, soldiery,
For present and shared silence. Jules, Marie.

[undated, 1884]

Mind! I will never become a *femme du monde* at the feet of a man of genius.

You must know that I don't hero-worship Monsieur Jules Bastien-Lepage. Take one of his works where he claims to have painted a scene at twilight. I defy you to look at it and tell me what time of day is depicted. The sky is grey and white, the church tower is black. The background is a veritable green that takes away the consistency of the figures. Truly, the lad needs guidance from my good self. (He should study my 'Umbrella', with its little working-girl, lonely in the rain.)

Yet he's not lacking in wisdom even if it is somewhat misplaced. I asked him how I should set about my choice of subjects and my treatment of them. 'Concentrate', he commanded. 'Upon one point.' How can I of all people do that? In me there is such an exuberance of ... abundance!

But what nonsense is thrown at us by the commentators. Jules and myself neither adopt nor renounce the Japanese, the Primitives etc. We are faithful to what we see. If our subject takes us into the street, we work in the street; if it's in the studio, we work in the studio. Anyone who is observant can remark the difference in light. To paint sailors at the coast *en plein air* and where the light is difficult; to paint urchins at the same street corner where one encounters them – is that following a 'system'?

I think he agrees with me that it is only when the subject is in repose that it can give us complete pleasure, allowing us to become absorbed in it, to penetrate it, to see it really living.

I will finish by thinking this little fellow quite handsome. I sing, I chatter, I laugh, and always the refrain comes round: Bastien-Lepage. It's not his person, nor his physique, and is hardly his talent ...

He believes that art is more than simply painting something *en plein air*. It is art even if it is a simple charcoal drawing.

Slava isskustvu!

21
At Damvillers – (I)

'That which we have apprehended intellectually may for long
remain unapprehended by us practically, emotionally
and spiritually.'
COUNT AUGUST VON WINOGRADOW
(1860-1918), *The Book of Blessed Platitudes* (1905)

An air of battle still lingered about these fields. Perhaps wafts of
smoke, which rose here and there near farmsteads, contributed to
this sensation. The odour was as acrid, perhaps, as that which once
combined with the hot reek of blood. This was a devastated country
only fourteen years past, but there was now a rediscovered (if
recent) prosperity. Folk might have wondered how the fate of
Europe could ever have been decided here, and if this swathe of
northern France would ever again mark the decline of one empire
and the emergence of another.

At Verdun, Mariya Konstantinovna Bashkirtseva enjoyed a
substantial breakfast, but was disappointed by the local water and
found herself longing for a nostalgic visit across the border to Spa.
A daft notion this was, for the Belgian resort was far to the north. In
any case, surely much more intense sensations awaited her in the
village of Damvillers.

Outside the inn in the station square, she boarded the
diligence. 'Ay, Maister Jules,' said the driver, when she indicated
her destination. 'Been daein weill for himsel, I hear, doun there in
the muckle toun tae. But his faither's vineyard – thon's even better.
Drink frae there, and ye'll never want anither drappie o watter in yer
life, ha, ha!'

Marie didn't want to encourage the man's garrulity, so she
kept quiet. That didn't stop him, so she heard more of the Bastien-
Lepage family history than she'd have bargained for, and had to
admit to herself that it was not quite devoid of interest to her.

The driver cracked his whip, and with an abrupt right-
angled turn into a dusty street, they arrived in the village square.

'There's mither Bastien.'

Marie saw a peasant woman, in late middle age, at the
village pump.

'Ay, ay, mither Bastien. There's a quinie here tae veesit ... yez.' The driver seemed to be stopping short of saying ' to visit your son'. Who was this chaperoneless young woman, he might have wondered, a fine sonsie young dame tae, and what for should she be up from Paris to this here neck of the woods?

The young woman was certainly enjoying to the full her chaperoneless condition – true, Mlle Carignan had been history for a good while, but Marie's realm of freedom seemed to be expanding every day now. Let her seize the time, while she still had it.

Mme Bastien laid down her pail and welcomed Marie with a motherly warmth. 'Jules wisna expeckin ye fir anither oor – he's ootby in the parks pentin, pentin. Ye canna haud him back frae his pentin! Och, dearie me, ye're a fine leddy, I maun ... I must apologeese tae ye for not talking fine myself. Excuse my manners, if ye please. We're a simple family, but we'll make sure you have a grand time with us.'

'Mme Bastien, I don't doubt it for a moment. I am very moved by your meeting me like this.'

Marie thought of other carriage-rides, thousands of kilometres to the east, and the decay that had met her when the wheels had seized up in the mud. The crumbling masonry, the moss and lichen ... but here was vigour, red, roundy people getting sweatily on with their life and their love. And why should they not, after the ravages of the war with the Prussians, doubtless still strong in their memories?

In the cottage Marie met Grandfather Lepage; family wines were brought, health was drunk. 'Miss, I hae heard tell o yer fiery watter o life, that they mak in your airt' ('That they make in your part of the world,' Mme Bastien softly interpreted).

Marie smiled, with sudden affection, at the old man.

'I'd gladly exchange it for this, sir.'

More clinking of glasses. It was a good start indeed.

Jules arrived. Marie had been a little nervous at the prospect of meeting him in his own part of the country. Now, the nervousness was faintly upon his side, but he seemed more relaxed than at their first encounter, and he kissed her hand with a grace that seemed too natural to have been tutored.

Marie was on the point of saying that that the gesture was worthy of a gentleman in the Ukraine, but she checked herself. She could love her brother no less for her long absence from him, but,

73

really, her Pavel – for all his dandified manners – was boorishness incarnate compared with this French peasant. Pavel (curse him!) would probably mock this French peasant-painter to his face. And for all his studied unconventionality, Pavel would probably berate her for lowering herself to her present company.

Well, Pavel wasn't here. Neither was her father (whom she'd have been ashamed to introduce to these delightful commoners). Let mother, too, remain in genteel ignorance down there in Nice. And as for the unlamented Mlle Carignan, what a laugh!

And she did laugh. Jules looked up, smiled, and also laughed, though he did not know why.

She had responded to his invitation to visit Damvillers for the period of the *fête*.

As well as the reputed wine, there were dishes such as *pôt au feu* and *soupe au lard*, far removed from the culinary experiences of Paris and Nice, let alone of Gavronzi. There was the honour of taking lunch with the village *maire*, causing Marie to exclaim to Jules: 'They can keep their Tsars and Tsaritsas and Tsarinas, their Napoleon IVs (poor fellow), their Dukes of ... H. ... - we have feasted today with the most courteous of potentates.'

'I dinna ... don't understand all that, Marie,' said Jules, 'but it sounded fair grand.'

'Thank you, Jules, for bringing me here.'

Jules wanted to reply that he thought she was a rare quine, but he thought he had better not.

In the evening there was dancing, and Jules remarked that the girl over there – the one who was the best in the village at waltzing – was the model for his painting 'The First Communion'.

'If I could match for her my musical art against your pictorial, I would play her my own repertoire of waltzes ... but you have no piano, and I can't play ... these instruments.'

Marie was here talking to herself as much as to Jules, who plucked up courage, said, 'Dinna mind that the nou', in a *sotto voce* tone – and as if he were in a ballroom, requested the next dance with her. Thereafter, he asked her to follow him to the end of the room where cakes and sweetmeats were available on a long table. On an impulse she touched his hand, let it go ... was jostled by a group of the menfolk, some of whom were reeling with the drink. M. the Curé was one of those revellers, in company with his favourite acolyte, who turned out to be one of the Lepage clan, a distant and somewhat disgraced cousin of Jules's.

'We must ... save the honour of France,' said the curé.

'Ye're richt, M'sieu, save honour France, g'rid of foreigners and fornicators. Hic.'

'God punished our country for its sins back in '70 ... We must redeem ourselves.'

'R'deem selves.'

'Your cousin there ... Jules, the artist fellow. Now, I don't ... I don't ...'

'You don't ...'

'I don't have time f'r this art nonsense normally ... it attracts and expresses the profane ...'

'The pr'fane.'

'But he, your cousin, that's Jules I'm talking about, Jules your cousin, he has honoured our national heroine, Joan of Domrémy ... a pure virgin, martyred by the foreigners for her defence of France.'

The cousin suddenly put by his stupor and became animated. 'As you say, M'sieu ... as you often say ... the Jews, the Freemasons ... kick 'em oot!'

'Steady on', said the curé, alarmed at what he'd started, though the sentiments were indeed his own.

'Thrash the Yids,' shouted the cousin, 'and save France!'

The cousin fell back into his stupor and slid under the table of desserts, pissing his trousers. Marie, horrified, forgetting that Jules was beside her, passed into a neighbouring room. She did not know where she was going. Jules hesitated, not knowing whether to follow her.

She had a vague recollection that she'd heard similar utterances in Gavronzi, as elsewhere in the Ukraine and Russia. But they'd be especially common in and around Gavronzi, surely. Pavel would have said such things, albeit with more finesse, her father too, with no finesse whatsoever. She had heard that Cossack bands were driving whole *shtetls* of Jews out of the Ukraine, and that they had the blessing of the Imperial powers for so purifying the motherland.

75

The Jews were heading for America ... why should she care about them? Because they had to leave their homes, because she, too, had to be on the move? Because, like them, she was uncertain of her future?

Why should she care about them? So, she was a woman and under the name of Pauline Morell she had condemned the exclusion of women who wished to become artists. But what did that have to do with the exclusion of the Jews?

Why should she care about them? That such utterances could be made in her native land, that was only to be expected ... what was so shocking hearing about them here, in France?

She wondered if she herself had said such things back home, and even written them in her journal, here in France ... but she had also met Jews, real Jewish women, among her *consœurs* in the Académie Rodolphe, among her comrades in the offices of *La Citoyenne* ...

The room in which she found herself was musty, and smelled as if too many corpses had been laid out here in their coffins, surrounded by candles. She caught a glimpse of herself in a cheval-glass, and screamed as if it had been a distorting mirror at a fair ...

Jules raised her gently, and conducted her to the care of his mother. In the morning she gave out that she 'had simply taken a turn' and that there was no need for a doctor. At that she tried in vain to suppress a cough. A red bubble appeared at the side of her mouth. Jules and his mother exchanged glances.

22
At Damvillers – (II) The Journal

[Undated, 1884]

My dreams, like my memories – can I ever distinguish between them? – become increasingly bizarre. I was in Menton again, with Mlle Carignan, and mother, and poor cousin Dina to whom I hardly ever give a thought. We had strolled as far as the Italian frontier, but didn't cross: I wished we had, for there were rocks there that I'd have loved to clamber upon and risk tumbling into the sea. We returned to the hotel by way of the steps and balustrades that face the harbour, almost got lost in the alleyways – how Mlle Carignan fussed, but I loved it! Mother did not so much fuss as fret, as she wished to meet two Russian ladies who were staying at the hotel. Princesses they were too. Mother is such a snob, a provincial child I would say.

It turned out that they had been warned about being seen with us, and we were snubbed. That did not stop me observing and eavesdropping upon them, sketch pad and pencil in hand. They would make excellent subjects, I thought. I could hide behind a palm.

So in the conservatory lounged these Mesdames Zassetska and Garshina, as they called themselves, sisters; they, too, had been on an expedition earlier in the day, and were glad to be relieved of Zassetska's children, whom their nurses were boring with Russian fairy stories. Garshina looked especially happy because she was flirting with a lanky young man with drooping moustaches. He didn't look healthy, coughed a lot and smoked more, albeit with a certain elegance, though he wasn't French – a northerner of sorts, English but not quite English – Scotch? – yet not sounding a bit like the Duke of H. I am rambling on.

A Russian lady, *d'un certain âge*, freed from a boorish Muscovite husband: there she is, among cushions and palms, with a charming foreigner ten years her junior. He was a writer, it seems, beginning to make a name for himself in Britain and America; he had written a pirate tale that was in the process of translation into – French. Aha, I thought, wait till it's translated into Russian, then Mme Garshina will really fall in love with you, won't she?

But he had a way with him, that's true. He promised Mme Garshina that he'd write a poem for her.

I wished he'd write a poem for me.

Did we ever meet, or did I just dream that we had? Perhaps he found me amusing. *Akh*, I was but a child then ... fifteen or so ... Curse Mesdames Zassetska and Garshina!

Here at Damvillers it is so peaceful. I thought for once that I should obey doctors' orders – whenever they order me south, I head north – and drink goat's milk. Jules had taken me to his meadow where he would often set his easel: on the way he introduced me to the animals, including a pretty little goat that liked to perch on a tree stump.

'She's a politician,' said Jules, 'and speaks from there. She wants the other animals to help her declare a Republic.'

'It would probably work better than a human Republic,' said I.

'Ay ... nae doot. But fit's ... what's certain is she can gie ye ... give you good milk.'

'Just what I need. Just what she needs too, to distract her from writing for the goat journals and causing trouble.'

He collected the milk: I fairly gulped it down, feeling its effects immediately.

'I'm now a New Woman, as they'd say across the water. But will you take some too, Jules? You look pale today. Shall we drink the same milk?'

In truth I thought it would make him a New Man. But I had embarrassed the poor fellow.

'Ay ... we'll drink the same milk, it micht help my stammach ...'

Then I saw a greyness upon his brow. He took out a handkerchief – perfectly white, no blood on it – and wiped his face, drank the milk, smiled, and I tell you, *this ugly little man became more beautiful than an angel.*

A painter? A poet, a psychologist, a God-like creator. Though his ways are far from God-like. I asked him how he did it – all these masterpieces and the acclaim they attracted.

He smiled. 'It's nae sae much paintin the parks ... the fields ... as ploughin them, whiles.'

'That's funny talk for you!'

'Nae really aw that funny. See oor lavvy ben the hoose ... sorry, our toilet in the house. You'll notice a wee proverb on the wall, that says DON'T JUST SIT THERE, THERE'S WORK TO BE DONE. That's all I'm daein. The daily darg. The day's work.'

'I work as hard as you, my friend, but my paintings don't attract the same attention. I'm just not as good as you.'

'I've had a head start. I'm ten year older than you, ken.'

I sighed. 'That's it. Time. When there are no other obstacles, time is terrible, draining, crushing, when it ought to be motivating and energising ...'

The greyness on his brow again.

'But I shouldna be mentioning lavatories, toilets. Not to a lady like yourself.'

'Why not? In my family we don't even acknowledge the existence of these places, so, my dear, your candour is extremely refreshing.' I chuckled at my mock-pomposity, following as it did my real-pomposity. The laughter brought on a spasm from my diaphragm to my chest, so I judged that a period of silence between us might be best.

We'll continue to drink milk from the same politic goat.

23

At Damvillers – (III) Masks and Mirrors

They head for the wood which had inspired Marie's 'Spring'. In that piece, a girl sits by the path, under an apple-tree in flower, meditates on ferns and violets; she is contemplating new love, perhaps. The sun settles on the scene. Marie wanted the spectator not only to see but also to hear – birds singing; butterflies flittering; bees buzzing – oh! *The wind in these branches, a brook babbling*, the girl's soft voicing of a name. Marie is losing that: her disease is slowly making her deaf. Jules has to raise his voice: not easy, as he is himself softly-spoken, and frailer by the day.

'You stop,' he says. 'Are we nae goin on? Dae ye want tae turn back?'

'Ay ... yes, Jules. In my picture the path loses itself in the distance. I'm not ready to explore it further ...'

She changed the subject by talking of his own pictures. He was reluctant to comment on them himself, and she sensed his embarrassment.

'Oh dear Jules, girls like me are ten-a-penny, as women or as artists. Well, I don't know if I really believe that, except when I'm with you. But "Pas Mêche" – "Nothing Doing" – yes, you fairly caught that young lad there. Standing by the lock, the open face and his work clothes and tools: I wondered, is he really as naïve as he looks? Only Jules Bastien-Lepage knows: for him the country, I know only the city. My impudent young fellows are together, conspiring – meeting, after all – your young fellows are alone. Each has an image all to himself – or herself ...

'Take "Going to School" – and a couple of years ago they found plenty to say about that, too, in their journals across the water! Yes, your paintings will find homes across the water; mine will be held only by French – and, if I'm lucky, in Russian – galleries, I know it.

'In that work, there she is, her large eyes confronting the spectator, inviting his compassion. How is she going to get through the day at school? How is she going to negotiate all her days at school? She's alone, all right ...'

' – Like your ain quinie in love in this wood – '

'Alone, alone, because look at the street, empty but for her, the windows and doorways dark and empty. Only one old body with a stick by the open gate at the right, but that person is merely looking at the girl who's looking at us. I see hope there, for that young lady, but also desolation.'

' – Again, that's affa like a description o your "Spring".'

'You don't need the city, Jules. I'd do the city if I could. I had only to see a bench in the Champs-Elysées, or even better, in a dreary suburb, and I'd say to myself: *that bench is connected with a romance, or a tragedy.*'

'I saw that in your "Autumn" … ye hae anither path, beside a river, and it vanishes in the mist – at the side o the path there's nae young woman, just a bench that's been overturned.'

'Death!'

'Daith.'

There is a silence for a few minutes. Marie continues to want to talk about his pictures, even as Jules would rather talk about hers.

'Your schoolgirl, Jules … people will say that she is me. I know it. That self-portrait I've been working on: I don't need to do it. You've caught me there in "Going to School".

'The most commonplace face can be made interesting by the addition of headwear, by an arrangement that is simple and also subtle. You like to drape a shawl around me. You did that this morning when we set out. You did that when … I took that turn at the *fête*. You're not conscious of it, but … you're being protective. You're also, when you do that, preparing me as the subject for your next masterpiece … clearly not for the first time – for before you even met me, you draped me in that hood which the schoolgirl wears … Oh, Jules, I am still going to school, and you are my teacher.'

The darling of European and American critics, the mentor of fine provincial painters for whom social realism is revolutionary, all the glowing epithets which Marie (and many others better-known than Marie) have bestowed upon him … Jules Bastien-Lepage is overwhelmed by what she is saying to him now.

'My teacher, not my mask, not my mirror.'

' – I'll hae tae tak a guid few gollops o goat's milk afore I'll can follae that! – '

81

'It's all clear to me, Jules. The mask is what I make for myself ... when I'm dancing in a square in Nice, when I'm trying to impress dreadful old Rodolphe and the rest of them at his Academy, when I'm writing as Pauline Morell (yes, that's me). The mask is an active thing, it's my activity that animates it.

'The mirror is passive. I didn't make it, I can't control it. Behind the mask, too, there is a real face, even though I may not be happy with that real face. But the mirror shows me my own absurdity, my own inadequacy, whether it reflects me masked or unmasked. And behind that mirror is – nothing. Just the dark, the void, panic – '

' – I'm thinkin you need – '

'And if the mirror shatters? What then?'

' – You need tae feenish thon self-portrait. Forget "Going to School".'

'As if I could!'

'Well, ye mebbe canna get my picter oot o your mind, but you should be trustin your ain vision ...'

She looks at him suspiciously.

'You're going to say, "Before it's too late." Yes, I'll do it. The face that will stare back at me from the completed canvas will stare back at a spectator a hundred years from now. He'll be a visitor to Nice, say, and he'll come across my portrait in the gallery, hung there quietly in an alcove by itself, alone, alone as usual. He'll remark the palette in my hand, the brushes, the harp in the background – oh! My music, my dear, dear music that's leaving me! – and he'll resolve to write a novel about me, poor fellow.'

' – Weill, I'll no could follae him there, I dinna hae the words like he will, like you yourself hae! You'll be the best o the three o us, wi your paintin and your writin, baith – '

'My large eyes will confront him out of the darkness, invite his compassion ... *Akh!* Enough of this. Me and my self-dramatisation. He'd be better off in a city of his own country, responding to your "Going to School" ... But here at Damvillers, and these lands around, I see nothing like the squalor of Gavronzi, all that mud and vodka.'

'Na, here it's mud and goat's milk.'

82

She stayed at Damvillers for a few days more than she had intended, ostensibly to restore herself after her 'turn'; then, it must be back to Paris and work, work.

'But you'll come and see me in Paris, in that muckle toun you all talk about here.'

'Ay ... juist telegraph and tell 's when ye're ready. Mebbe your portrait'll be dune by then.'

'If only.'

Jules stumbled on a piece of rock that projected from the rough track over the field. She herself had tripped on the exposed root of a tree. In either case, the one alternately supported the other with a hand to the arm, gently but feebly.

'We'll show them,' said Marie. 'Imperialists here and in Russia, Republicans, Nihilists, the Salon, philistines, bankers, Freemasons, the Church, the Jews ...'

Her hand rose to her mouth, but no blood came. 'All those who do too much and never look inside themselves ... who never look inside anything except their safes.

'I'm jabbering on. My apologies, Jules.'

'Ye're juist a quinie aff tae the school.'

'Yes. But no more alone.'

24
In the Buttes-Chaumont

The Park of the Buttes-Chaumont does not so much imitate nature as parody it.

Once the site was a quarry, and there were many who could tell you how much of Paris was built out of it, and where. Abandoned, it became the abode of aged drinkers and whores, and there followed years of sorry fuddlings and fumblings in the crevices left by the stonebreakers. Then came a transitional period as the purple-fleshed wrecks were scoured out by the gendarmerie, even as the workmen arrived to construct a park for the new bourgeois residents of the quarter. The turning point was the final swearing-match between the last non-bourgeois resident and the gardeners' lads, who took great delight in a sport unparalleled for the energy expended on it by both sides. The former Buttes-Chaumonters continued to fester and bleed under the bridges of the Seine. Meanwhile, Napoleon III's freshly-minted suburbanites allowed their scampering children to explore the caverns so recently occupied by raving dragons. Parasols were twirled, moustachios fingered as human affections leisurely crossed marital boundaries. Little boats could be rowed around the precipitous island that had been created from the old workings. A system of pumps ensured that the 'lake' was always safely free of foreign bodies. But not of domestic bodies. For there developed one melancholy counterfoil to this corner of Second Empire utopia: the longer of the two bridges connecting the mainland to the island became known as the Pont des Suicides.

The old and infirm could enjoy the park because of generous railing; moreover, flanking the paths that climbed the island as well as those linking the upward sweep of the park to the north and east, there were balustrades formed to resemble the criss-crossing of roots and branches – so that, in addition to the real trees and shrubs, there was stonework that convincingly resembled wood. This is a forest, it all seemed to say, only it's not.

The underground railway sliced through the north-western sector of the park, so you could relax with your coffee or mineral water at one of the rustic chalets while enjoying the music and the reek of the capital's confident interconnections. There was, of course, the unfortunate interruption to the park's services when the Communards held out here in '70, but once order was quickly restored, each spent bullet, each drop of blood and each fragment of tissue was meticulously located and removed. Even those lingering languid suicides – though they couldn't be stopped altogether – were expeditiously collected and disposed of. You couldn't have the place cluttered up with *poètes maudits*, dead or alive (or in between, most of them, God help them.)

Perversely, though, this philistine paradise was destined to attract an even more insolent breed of arty types. They'd call themselves Surrealists, and it wasn't a painter but a poet who came up with that term. (My God, they were all in it together.) So these fellows staked their claim to this place, even as real people continued to play in the park and ignore them as much as possible before calling the police. Not content with the Buttes-Chaumont, the new obsessives found a counterpart craze in the South, south-east of Lyon to be precise, when they learned of the activity of one M. Cheval. This postman of the realm, every day of his work from 1879 up to 1912, and during his seaside holidays, collected stones and shells and built them into a gigantic heap which he called his Palais Idéal. As at Buttes-Chaumont, there were gorges, grottoes and alcoves a-plenty, walkways that looked like they'd been formed by centuries of erosion until you examined them close up; everywhere you encountered juxtapositions of the banal and the exotic, the whole a monument to the unexpected and (if you please!) the subversive.

That was to come. During the late summer of 1884 a young man and a young woman were strolling through the Buttes-Chaumont during a rare break from their habitual – and ever-intensifying – industry. Each knew that the other was dying. The young woman admired the young man's work more than she admired her own. She told him that he was as great as M. Victor Hugo. He laughingly protested that M. Hugo was very old and might even die before they did – and what would happen then?

Marie replied that she was minded to attempt more work 'in the Impressionist manner', having once had doubts about such practice. Akh, but even Impressionism had had its day, she felt; France was no longer interested, though she had heard that America now was. She recalled that at Rodolphe's *atelier* the American students were slow to catch on to new developments, but once they did, they raged into them like terriers with a bone which they'd just found.

Jules smiled. 'The Americans are as conservative as we are in their ain way. What you say is nae doubt true, but they still interview me for their illustratit magazines. And just wait – sorry, no, *soon*, they'll be queuing up at your studio ...'

'After I'm gone.'

'Na: fame – or rather reputation – plays strange tricks with time: dinna worry.'

'If only,' she sighed, 'reputation could indeed control time, not the other way round.'

'Noo, that would lead tae some kinna strange movements in art!'

'We won't be there to witness them – let alone be a part of them ...'

...I look up at the buildings surrounding the park –
the high domes, the interplay of wrought iron and
glass ... they take on fantastic shapes and I feel nearer
to my own country: east of Berlin and Vienna there may rise
odd efflorescences - towers of scarlet ringed with small
shield-like windows and sculpted female shapes clasping hands
around their upper rim – and down below, swirling metal
shapes beguiling each cream-coloured storey as, at street level,
the people queue for food ...
It is late afternoon and these bulbous lamp-posts
around the park will soon be lit, and the whole arrondissement
will become a shimmering dream ...

'There's the waterfall aneath the rock, Marie ... come ben and we'll tak a turn across the stepping stones.'

Akh, Jules, these are small pleasures, of no use to the work
remaining to us ... and yet how can we tell that the merest
triviality may not stimulate a future work of depth and
grandeur? Was it not over a coffee at the Retiro, as we saw
the gypsies dancing, that my autumn in Spain was gathered
into my consciousness – the labyrinth of Toledo, cathedral,
mosque and synagogue, the Alhambra's proud display of
colour and intricacy, the streams bubbling there between the

violets, Velasquez! Ribera! ... What a rebirth that was for
me, a northerner who knew the south but who had to
venture even further south! One sip of coffee it was, as I
draped my arm over a battered round-backed chair ... they
lit the lanterns as twilight fell, and I saw distant lights with
haloes ... why do they claim that blue is the colour of cold?

'I have completed my self-portrait, Jules. My gaze awaits
those who will come after! You will be one of them, Jules.'
'I'll be there even if I need help to bring me there.'
'I, too, will need help soon ...'

... So now I can press on with my resolution at the
Retiro: Mary the Mother of God and Mary Magdalen at the
tomb of Jesus. All others had departed from the sepulchre,
after the stone was rolled before it; only these two women
remained. Can there be a scene more compassionate, more
sublime? Will I be able to complete it? Should I tell Jules?

'Marie, thon image ye were workin on ...'
'Jules!'

Had I told him already?

'It was a burlesque sort o subjeck.'

Ah, he means something else: it was to be the interior
of a studio, the artist having departed, and the model
lounging on a chair, smoking, contemplating a skeleton
opposite, also seated, and with a pipe in its mouth ...

'Abandon that: ye've got mair vital stuff within ye ... work
on that instead.'

He knows ... he has an intuition. I shan't mention the
two women at the sepulchre, I'll just get on with it ...
Here we are at the Pont des Suicides ... another man,
another woman, might join hands and leap from here ...
not us: we want more life, more life, not less of it. The
paths slope up and down across the island, in and out of

grottoes ... I'm tired, I'm weak, will I make it to the
summit? I must be strong, for Jules's sake, that he can
absorb strength from me ... oh no I have a headache
coming on we should have stopped at the kiosk for a
seltzer I must not cough he will see the blood

'Marie, let me tak your arm – here's a bench, set doun and byde some.'

No, I must get through this down into the grottoes
they are not real caves they are profoundly silly such a
view from their openings but nothing more romantic
than Paris below and beyond to-ing and fro-ing at its
business nursemaids and babies by the lake these rough
steps taking us further down into the rock the
catacombs of Kiev it's getting darker each cell with a
monk inside crossing himself before the ikon an even
bigger cell like the church to the chapels a coffin
there the acrid smell of three candles a young girl in
white lying there and mirrors mirrors in the labyrinth
we'll lose ourselves in here

Gospodin pomilul

It is hot in here I have risen like Rusalka from the
lake and am Snyegúrochka even as Mizgir with his
dear rough ways embraces me the clouds part and I
melt I was the blood woman who toiled too long in
the shadows white and red white and red

Kolokoli, kolokoli

Marie and Jules emerged into a path winding back up the rock towards the island's summit, where rose the small temple, the monopteros with its panorama of the northern stretch of the city. As they approached it, for the first time Marie seized Jules's hand, led him between the columns to the centre of the structure –

'I want us to be part of all this. I want all this to be part of us.'

'Whit's got intae ye, wumman?'

'I don't know. I felt like we were going to leap together into the heart of a vast joke.'

'It wouldna be very funny bein scratched by these shrubs and battered by these sticky-oot rocks. I dinna fancy sinkin intae thon bit lake, forby.'

'We can't go any higher than this spot.'

'Na, but we'll could gang a lang wey lower.'

'Unless we climb to the roof of the temple.'

'Ay, and brak oor necks.'

'We're broken enough as it is.' Her laughter turned to weeping; still grasping his hand, she brought him nearer. They remained in silence. The sun was down, she hadn't melted, no-one else was about at this hour –

Jules! No – help, help ... my God we're alone and
Jules, Jules ... what do I do?

He had clutched his stomach: a violent spasm, intense pain. She must leave him here, run across the western bridge, out of the park and into the nearest restaurant, just opening, to demand that someone find a doctor. One of the two waiters was sent to an apartment nearby. The other remained, brought water, and sought to calm her.

'Thank you. Thank you. It is so urgent.' She gulped down the water, made a choking sound, and there was a froth of blood upon her lips.

'M. Meylan will attend to your friend, Madame ... and then, if you will permit me, to yourself.'

September 17, 1884

When I am weak, Jules visits me; when I am weak, I visit him.

Few days pass now but I am tormented by the memory of my father. He died at Gavronzi in June, aged only fifty or so ... and I was not there. At the time I thought little of my loss: I would be glad of fifty years for myself. That isn't going to happen, so I must think only of him and how it might have been better between us. He was a monster, and in that respect he resembled me. I smile at certain of his utterances, as when he compared mother to a hen which would try to cover its little ones with its wings. Paul ... Pavel inherits the estate, such as it is, but for all his dissolute ways he will manage it well, perhaps even make it prosper. The old hag Alyona was right: Pavel will be nothing more than a gentleman farmer. We'll not be a whole constellation together ... dear brother ... little brother ... (*little* brother, the great languid lank of him!)

We'll not be anywhere together now.

But I'm not alone, after all. Dina looks after me – that gentle daughter of scapegrace Uncle Georges, poor cousin Dina to whom I've given little thought in recent times. Looking through my journal, I see that I have barely mentioned her: once or twice in my record of the Spanish journey, and that is it. Now I'm dependent on her during the months remaining to me.

So she cares for me, and I – when I can – care for Jules.

...

The poor fellow has needed an extra pillow, so I brought one for him. From my handkerchiefs, I made him a new pillow-case and embroidered a large J upon it. The doctor ordered him to take a certain dubious-looking meat: if his gorge rises at it, I eat some of it in front of him, by way of encouragement. When we are all able to meet in the Bois, with our respective entourages, I drape my black shawl around myself; as you know, it pleases him greatly. I stand against the trees in their early autumn glory. Then the rain comes down, and Jules smiles as my hair uncurls and I survey the scene with the confidence of a sixteen-year-old 'quine'.

Approaching thirty, but with no hope of reaching it, I ask: who am I, or rather who are we?

There are two of me: one who lives and acts, not always thinkingly, and the other who coldly spectates and observes: even so were the Lilliputians, with their absurd obsessions, looked upon by Gulliver.

But Marie B. is an enigma to herself. I am the French 'Monsieur' Bashkirtseff, to use the title conferred on me by an idiot at the Salon, but do I now wish any longer to be French? France is charming, amusing etc. but apart from Géricault and Bastien-Lepage, it produces no art that could be called profound. As for the music, there are perfectly crafted operas – and when I could sing, I loved certain arias: 'Connais-tu le pays ...' from M. Thomas's *Mignon*, because I loved its celebration of the South – but where are the symphonies? I corresponded unsatisfactorily with M. de Maupassant, and no doubt my detractors will make much of that, and I have of course sought to emulate M. Zola, I've made that pretty clear; but the coming man is surely one of our own aristocrats, Count Tolstoy. Yes, he is white-bearded now, and denounces his own youth, but in reading *War and Peace* I am aware of both the historian and the prophet. If we Russians reject one faith, we need to replace it with another (so much for the 'nihil' in Nihilism!), and the Count will be echoed down through the twentieth century.

So I am also – and if only more so! – Mariya Konstantinovna Bashkirtseva. Had I lived, one of my many (too many!) ambitions would have been to present the Russian landscape to the world. Others will do that, painters who have never left Russia as I did. Whenever I have extolled the vistas around Damvillers, Jules has appeared puzzled: the folk around here, he says, don't admire landscape, it's their place of work. The dear prig, the philistine that he is! I have painted my own places of work, the fervent muddle of the Académie Rodolphe and the clutter of my studio; and besides, Jules has never been to Russia, he does not know its power ... it's too late now.

I am descended from a race of nomads, the Bashkirs: they belonged to the east, and came west. I have flitted east, I have flitted west, and have wondered where I really belong. I am now certain

91

that I am not, after all, French; perhaps not, after all, Russian Grand or Russian White but Russian Little – I am Ukrainian.

October 1, 1884

Emile, Jules's brother, has tenderly installed him in an armchair – the poor little fellow looks quite lost into it, with those skeletal legs of his tapering off into a mound of cushions. His family are more loving to me than ever before: I had saved his life in the Buttes-Chaumont. Ah, what little life there was left to save!

That is wrong; when the passion seizes him ...

As today, when I called round (with Dina's help). For me, first of all, it was the reminder of Belgium during his conversation: our early flittings, me, mother, Dina and Carignan, from Ostend to Spa and back to Ostend again, not that the good waters saved my throat and lungs.

Jules had been in Ghent to receive a prize from his admirers up there, and with his usual aversion to fuss, had made sure that he could escape for half an hour or so. He found himself blissfully alone in a bookshop in an alley behind the town hall and square. Browsing through the boxes of pamphlets and exhibition catalogues, enjoying a lack of intellectual purpose, he was a little irritated when the bookseller pressed upon him the latest local literary sensation. It was a novel called *Art in Exile*, about a Ghent writer who decides to leave the town for Paris. This fellow is weary of the provincialism of his native streets: he has no-one to talk to, he is a swan among geese, etc. etc. He lives with his aged mother who mutters only pieties learned from her priest; tradesmen are the only callers, intent on settling their bills which have remained unpaid because our writer has been so absorbed in his masterpiece.

After obligingly reading the first two chapters or so, Jules returned the volume to the bookseller, who appeared quite baffled, not quite as baffled, though, as Jules was by the concept of art in exile. You just get on with it, he said, in that way he has of speaking in dialect and forgetting that he's talking to me. If I understand him right, it was just like ploughing the fields: a duty. It was also not like ploughing the fields: a pleasure.

Art in exile: I don't know if I understand it either. I suspect M. Baudelaire started it all, but after him the notion was vulgarised by his more vocal disciples. Perhaps, though, Hubertine Auric and her circle have an inkling of it as something of real significance, yet apart from my own Pauline Morell, the good comrades of *La Citoyenne* were not much vexed with art as such. But what of those of our own people – if the Jews are of our people – the luckier ones who arrive at New York in one boatload after another these days, and sing of their tears by the waters of the American Babylon, determined never to forget Jerusalem? Or so *les citoyennes* used to tell me in so many words, as also one or two of the models at the Académie Rodolphe.

In France women with pince-nez are regarded as ridiculous. (I recall how I mocked poor Mademoiselle Carignan, though of course she fully deserved it). In Russia women with pince-nez are regarded as dangerous. If they are poets or painters, eventually they must leave for the likes of Schlangenbad or Baden-Baden; otherwise, it's the Peter and Paul Fortress for them, or somewhere far north and east of Irkutsk, or at best the pinioned stance upon a trapdoor. That much I learn from Dina, in whispers; she exhorts me not to say anything of this to mother, or to write it down.

Russia's triad: God, nation, people. Some believe in all three and consider them a unity. Others judge the 'nation' to have been corrupted by the hypocritical rhetoric of the authorities, against whom the people must rise up, God or no God. Dina does not need to tell all me that: I can work it out for myself.

Now M. Hugo – he was an exile. He returned to us, but he is well over eighty, and will soon leave us again.

October 17, 1884

Jules now seems detached from the earth: he is already floating above us. There are days when I am like that. You see folk, they speak to you and you respond, but you're no longer on earth: it's a tranquil, painless indifference you have, as in a dream induced by opium.

Bastien is dying.

I'm only going to his apartment from habit. It's only his shadow which is there, and I am half a shadow myself. What's the point?

He doesn't particularly feel my presence. I'm useless. I'm not able to put the light into his eyes. He's content just to see me, that's all.

Yes, he's dying, and I can accept that. I'm indifferent to it, even barely conscious of it. It's all passing away. I myself will be buried sometime during 1885.

Nobody seems to love *everything* as I did: art, music, painting, books, society, dress, luxury, excitement, calm, laughter, sadness, nonsense, love, cold, sunshine; all the seasons, all atmospheric conditions, the serene steppes of Russia and the mountains around Naples and Nice; the snow in winter, the rain in autumn (ah! That overturned bench), spring and its sillinesses, the quiet days of summer and the beautiful nights with the brilliant constellations ... It is all sublime, and if only I could have captured it all on poor canvas: could anyone have done that? Jules, even?

I wanted to see everything, to have everything, to embrace everything, to *be* everything if not quite everyone ...

The last faint signs of Jules's care for me: the scoundrel even tries to lean forward and button up my coat, insists on protecting me ...

'Oh, if I could paint,' says he.

And I too ... and also continue to write ...

I have outlines for two novels and a *History of the Caesars*, as well as the scenario for a drama ... my *History of Famous Women* will remain unfinished. Is it not all so absurd?

October 20, 1884

The weather is magnificent. But Bastien comes here instead of to the Bois. He can barely walk; Emile, his brother, holds him under each arm. Dear, devoted Emile: he carries Jules on his shoulders up to the third floor. Dina is equally committed to me. These two days my bed has been in the salon, but as that room is large and partitioned by screens (oh the Japanese eye – could we learn from it?) ... and by that piano, silent now ... no-one would notice ... my bed ... why should I lie here in the shadows, there's work to be done ... I am walking up a gentle slope in a northern city ... on the horizon, to the right, there are stables ... to the left, an embankment topped with bare, spindly trees in silhouette ... but it is getting dark and I can't see the end of our path ... at last I grasp Jules's hand ... to my right I feel the presence of my father, sadly nodding assent ... but in truth ... it is too difficult for me to climb the stairs ...

Epilogue:
The Apotheosis of Mariya Konstantinovna Bashkirtseva

The aipple-tree blumed i the gairden,
blumed and shrunkled:
the mither spylt her dochter,
spylt her, brocht her oot –
then left her by her lane.
Whaur are you, mither?
Look doun frae your hichts,
on your bairn,
on your ain dear dochter,
look, mither dear!
Gin this be your dochter
in her new jirkin
wi the bonnie threid-wark?
Gin this be your dochter
Wi a silken reebon
braidit in her hair;
wi a gowden geegaw
roond her cauld-white neck?
But hersel, your dochter,
canna be sae bonnie:
wha's the lad will love her,
love her and enbrace her?
(After Yakov Polonsky, freely)

Marie Bashkirtseff, painter who 'triumphed' at the Salon, died of tuberculosis on October 31, 1884, aged twenty-six. Jules Bastien-Lepage, painter fêted in France and abroad as master of *plein-air* rural realism, died of stomach cancer on December 10, 1884, aged thirty-six. His brother Emile, the architect, designed the monuments in Passy Cemetery for both Jules and Marie. Marie's monument has been compared to an eastern kiosk, or to a small Orthodox church.

Jules was too ill to attend Marie's funeral, whose arrangements were meticulously overseen by her mother, draped as she was in the Orthodox style of black head-dress and robes. The ceremonies began in the room where Marie had died.

With the saints let the soul of thy deceased servant Mariya Konstantinovna, O Lord, rest in peace, and keep her in everlasting remembrance.

Everyone knelt and touched the floor with their foreheads. At the same moment, in Gavronzi, Pavel and the servants kissed the soil of Ukraine.

All the mirrors in Marie's apartment were shrouded, according to the Orthodox custom: this is to prevent the deceased's spirit from seeing its reflection and becoming trapped.

At the cemetery the printed prayer was placed in the folded hands of the dead Mariya. All present kissed these hands. Wine and oil were sprinkled with incense upon the body; had they been in Gavronzi, earth would have been scattered upon it. Marie's mother suddenly became aware of this and interrupted the service:

'She loved France, and France loved her. Let my dear daughter be blessed with the dust of her adopted country.'

They all obeyed this instruction, including the priest.

The chants ceased, people dispersed. The mother insisted on being taken to Marie's studio, deserted and dusty. She allowed others to sort out the paintings, though she was arrested by sudden sight of the portrait of Pavel. Torn between admiration of her daughter's skill and disapproval of the depiction of such an impudent, immoral son, she grunted and passed on. (*The trouble with that boy*, she thought to herself, *is that he is too Russian, just like his father.*) The portraits of common people, of studio models and street urchins – she could not distinguish between the two categories – did not interest her. Briefly she wondered if Marie's final self-portrait should be shrouded, then she decided that it was not a mirror, only a painting. She must not delay. She was looking, above all, for papers, having suspected that her daughter did not keep all the manuscripts of her journal in the apartment. Whatever of these she found, she placed in a leather bag, while feeling vexatious at her chronic inability to decipher (and therefore control) her daughter's scrawl; there shot through her, also, the terror that perhaps there might somewhere be other manuscripts, letters, notebooks, even parts of the journal, that could be inflammatory and untraceable.

Then in a dark corner, she discovered copies of *La Citoyenne*. When no-one else was looking, she quickly stuffed them into the bag, intending to burn them.

Those who visit the cemetery at Passy may peer into the interior of Mariya's tomb. If a few candles are flickering there, they may discern what appears to be a mural. It is very indistinct, but is said to depict two draped female figures, in mourning, to the right of a large rock.

The writer who had dominated the century, Victor Hugo, died on May 22, 1885, aged eighty-three. During the night of May 31, his coffin lay on a grand catafalque beneath the Arc de Triomphe, protected by a rota of twelve poets.

The funeral took place the following day. The Parisians left their jobs and their pleasures to accompany the body to the grave. The city was also full of people who had arrived from the provinces and the colonies to pay their respects. A novelist, Maurice Barrès, asked himself 'Is this a fair? No – it is humanity around a coffin ... Paris was filled with the aromas of its love for a relic... How many women gave themselves to lovers, to strangers, with a burning fury to become the mothers of immortals?'

Copies of Hugo's photograph were touted in the streets. There were brass bands, speeches, faintings and even deaths in the crowd, as the procession made its way to the Pantheon. The church had to be 'unconsecrated' for this day only, for the great man had stated in his will:

'I give fifty thousand francs to the poor. I wish to be carried to the cemetery in the hearse of the paupers. I refuse the prayers of all churches. I ask for prayers from all living souls. I believe in God.'

The lamp-posts were bedecked with tricolours. A small number of anarchists attempted to wave red flags but they received the swift ministrations of the police. Surrounded by people on the Boulevard Saint-Michel, Hubertine Auric mourned alone. Her temperamental apprehension was, as always, at odds with her obligatory optimism. She had chosen not to join her comrades on this day; nevertheless she wondered what had become of Pauline Morell.

In the September 18, 1886, edition of *Le Figaro*, the poet Jean Moréas published his Symbolist manifesto. Henceforth, the artist must apprehend reality by means of intuition and express it by means of allusion. He must not purvey information; he must not declaim; he must not attempt objective description. His colleague, Mallarmé, maintained that 'to *name* an object is to suppress three-quarters of the enjoyment of the poem, which derives from the pleasure of step-by-step discovery: to *suggest*, that is the dream.' The painter and lithographer, Odilon Redon, summed up his own practice: 'the visible at the service of the invisible.' Better the evocation of the unconscious than the solution of a social problem.

August 2007

As expected, the Baltic is calm, and the dusty, oppressive heat – so evoked by Dostoevsky in *Crime and Punishment* – is everywhere throughout St Petersburg.

Below a dome of glass and wrought-iron, the *style moderne* angels of the Singer Building overlook the crowd in the Nevsky Prospekt. In the restored bookshop someone has put on a CD of lugubrious lyricism – Nataliya's 'Nightingale' aria from Tchaikovsky's *The Oprichnik*. Appropriately enough, a middle-aged man browses through the books on ornithology, and gazes at images of gulls, cranes, ravens. In the café a group of young foreigners, all men, are sitting in the armchairs. There is a good view of that very south-European Cathedral, of Our Lady of Kazan, with its cupola and colonnades, but the young men are too busy talking to take much notice. One of them stubs out his cigar at the request of the waitress, who speaks a little English and briefly explains the new rule. He responds by trying to flirt with her.

His friends, apparently oblivious to this, keep on talking.

'So you guys, you call them ladybirds. That is so totally cool.'

'Yes, well, but there are no ladybirds here. Except for her' – indicating the waitress.

'Back home we call them ladybugs.'

The young waitress, almost twenty, doesn't smile. There has been a rumpus between one of the older girls and their boss, and the atmosphere is tense, though only one or two customers remark on this. The twenty-year-old has a determined set of the mouth; her eyes are red-rimmed, staring, and she feels a headache coming on. She brings the young foreigners their coffee, returns to the counter, places her fingers on her forehead and into her clasped-up hair when she thinks no-one is looking. She glances around the bookshelves, at the glowering reproduced portraits of Russia's writers, composers

98

and painters on the café walls, looks across the avenue to the traffic, the shoppers, the Cathedral, wonders how she will negotiate her way through art school.

THE END

Marie Bashkirtseff: as others have seen her

'Mlle Bashkirtseff attracts and repels alternately, perhaps repels as much as she attracts.'
> William Ewart Gladstone, British statesman and four times Prime Minister, reviewing Maire's Journal for the periodical *The Nineteenth Century* in 1889.

'Have you yet seen "Le Journal de Marie Bashkirtseff"? I am reading it, a wonderful and delightful book, and the cosmopolitan atmosphere of it puts me into feverish unrest. It is absurd that I should be mouldering here in a Yorkshire village; it is scandalous waste of life, when already I have wasted so many years.'
> George Gissing, English novelist, in a letter to his German friend Eduard Bertz, June 22, 1890.

'Marie Bashkirtseff [...], without any compulsion from circumstances, made herself a highly skilled artist by working ten hours a day for six years. Let anyone who thinks that this is no evidence of self-control just try it for six months.'
> George Bernard Shaw, *The Quintessence of Ibsenism* (1891).'

'ALGERNON Do you really keep a diary? I'd give anything to look at it. May I?
'CECILY Oh no. *(Puts her hand over it.)* You see, it is simply a very young girl's record of her own thoughts and impressions, and consequently meant for publication. When it appears in volume form I hope you will order a copy.
****
'GWENDOLEN [...] I never travel without my diary. One should always have something sensational to read in the train.'
> Oscar Wilde, *The Importance of Being Earnest* (1895).

'I have noticed that Ukrainian women tend to be either laughing or crying; there is no intermediate mood.'
Anton Chekhov, 'The Man in a Case' (1898).

'To-day in my walk I found a cabbage.
'It lay in a corner of the hedge. Cruel boys had chased it there with stones.
'It was dead when I lifted it up.
'Beside it was an egg.
'It too was dead. Ah, how I wept –
****
'How can I bear it? Alexis is to take me to Petersburg, and he has bought a beautiful house in the Prospekt, and I am to live in it with him, and we are to be rich, and I am to be presented at the Court of Nicholas Romanoff and his wife. Ah! Is it not dreadful?'
Stephen Leacock, Canadian humourist and parodist, in his 'Sorrows of a Super Soul, or, the Memoirs of Marie Mushenough (translated, by Machinery, Out of the Original Russian)', collected in his *Nonsense Novels*, 1911.

'When at sixteen she visited her father in Russia she packed, with thirty gowns, Plato, Dante, Ariosto, Shakespeare, some English novelists, and the Encyclopedia.'
Virginia Moore, *Distinguished Women Writers*, 1934.

'What woman essentially lacks today for doing great things is forgetfulness of herself, but to forget oneself it is first of all necessary to be firmly assured that now and for all the future, one has found oneself.'
Simone de Beauvoir, *The Second Sex*, 1949.

Details of the Paintings Cited in the Novel

To see further details of these works please visit the publisher's website at www.midoil.co.uk, where appropriate links are indicated.

Marie Bashkirtseff

AUTOPORTRAIT À LA PALETTE / SELF-PORTRAIT WITH A PALETTE
c. 1883/84.
Musée de Beaux-Arts (Jules Chéret), Nice

LE MEETING / THE MEETING
1884
Musée d'Orsay, Paris

LE PRINTEMPS / SPRING
1884
Russian Museum, St Petersburg

L'AUTOMNE / AUTUMN
1883
Russian Museum, St Petersburg

Jules Bastien-Lepage (1848-1884) 10 years older than Marie B,

PAS-MÊCHE / NOTHING DOING
1882
National Gallery of Scotland, Edinburgh

JEANNE D'ARC / JOAN OF ARC
1879
Metropolitan Museum of Art, New York

GOING TO SCHOOL
1882
Aberdeen Art Gallery, Scotland

Jean Béraud

LA PÂTISSERIE GLOPPE / THE PASTRY-SHOP 'GLOPPE'
1889 [sic; cited anachronistically in the novel]
Musée Carnavalet, Paris

Wordleet

All words glossed are Scots unless otherwise indicated (Fr. = French; Ger. = German; Rus. = Russian).

aa	all
aff	off
affa	awful; very
aiblins	perhaps
ain	own
aipple	apple
anely	only
arrondissement (Fr.)	district of Paris
aw	all
aye (fir aye)	forever
ayont	beyond
bairn	child
baith	both
baur	except (bar)
ben	inside
Berendei, Tsar	a character in the story, and opera, of *The Snow Maiden* (see *Snyegúrochka*, below)
braidit	braided
brak	break
breeks	trousers
brocht her oot	brought her out
byde	stay; remain
cannae	can't
cauld	cold
c'est dégoûtant (Fr.)	it's disgusting, gross
chaipel	chapel
che bella regina! (Niçois dialect / Italian continuum)	What a beautiful queen!
cowpit	(1) ruined; (2) screwed, had sex with
daein	doing
daith	death
darg	arduous work; toil
deid	dead
didnae	did not

dinna	don't
dinnae	don't
dochter	daughter
drappie	drop
enbrace	embrace
en plein air (Fr.)	see *plein air, en*
fa	who
faraboots	whereabouts
feart	afraid
femme du monde (Fr.)	society woman
ferlie	strange, eerie
fit	what
fly (on the fly)	surreptitiously; craftily
flyting	arguing, variously in a vehement and / or bantering manner
forby	moreover
gallus	spirited; possessing chutzpah
gang	go
garred	made; caused
gie	give
gien	gave
gin	if
Goad	God
goat	got
gollops	gulps
Gospodin pomilul (Rus.)	God, be our help
gowden geegaw	golden trinket
hae	have
heid-yin	head one
hichts	heights
hüre	whore
huvtae	have to
ilkawhaur	everywhere
jirkin	blouse
jyle	jail
kinna	kind of
kolokoli (Rus.)	church bells
lane, by her	alone
lang	long
lavvy	lavatory
loady	load of
lounie	boy; boyish

lowpt	leapt
lugs	ears
lume	penis
mair	more
Märchen (Ger.)	folk-tales, fairy stories
maun	must
Mizgir (Rus.)	young peasant in the story of the Snow Maiden
muckle toun	big town or city
nae	not
naebody	nobody
nane	none; no-one
nou	now
ootby	outside; over there
pentin	painting
picters	pictures
pince-nez (Fr.)	spectacles which are worn perched on the nose
pittin	putting
plein air, en (Fr.)	in the open air, out of doors
poètes maudits (Fr.)	doomed poets (the phrase was used by Verlaine as the title of a book of essays [1884] on French poets)
Pruscos (Fr., colloquial)	Prussians
puir	poor
quine	lass, girl
reebon	ribbon
reid	red
richt	right
rossigno che volà (Niçois dialect /Italian continuum)	nightingale which is flying
Rusalka (Rus.)	Slavonic female water-spirit
saftie	softy
scunnert	disgusted
sel-murtherers	self-murderers: suicides
shaddas	shadows
shair	sure
shrunkled	shrivelled
shtetls (Yiddish)	formerly Jewish villages in eastern Europe and Russia
siller	money (silver)

Slava iskusstvu! (Rus.)	Glory to art!
Snyegúrochka (Rus.)	Snow Maiden, in Russian folklore and an opera [1882] by Rimsky-Korsakov
sonsie	buxom
sowel	soul
spae-wife	fortune-teller
speerit	spirit
spylt	spoiled
stishie	fuss; rumpus
stoap	stop
style moderne (Fr.)	Russian art nouveau / Jugendstil
sympa (Fr.)	sympathetic; on 'our' side; nice
tae	(1) to; (2) too
taen	taken
tak	take
telt	told
thon	that
thread-wark	thread-work; embroidery
tozie	dirty; dishevelled
travail à deux (Fr.)	two people working together
Tsar Berendei	see *Berendei, Tsar*
versts (Rus.)	Russian measurement of distance
wad	would
waw	wall
wan	one
weill	well
wey	way
yin	one
yince	once
yird	bury